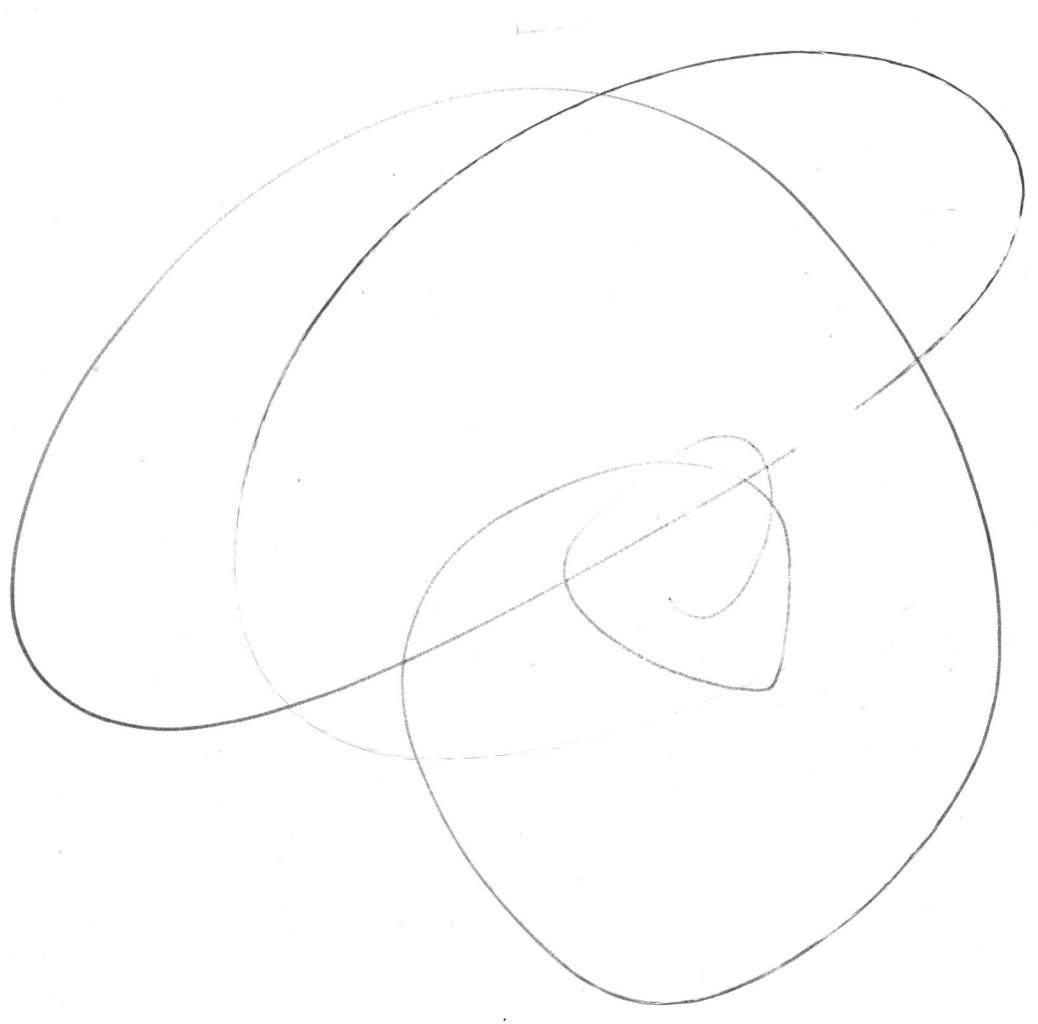

366 Goodnight Stories

366 Goodnight Stories

WRITTEN BY

MIROSLAV ŽILINA

ILLUSTRATED BY

MIROSLAV RADA

CATHAY BOOKS

First published 1983 by
Cathay Books Limited
59 Grosvenor Street
London W1

Translated by Stephen Finn
Graphic design by Přemysl Pospíšil
This edition copyright © Artia, Prague 1983
ISBN 086178 230 5
Printed in Czechoslovakia by Svoboda, Prague
1/20/05/51-01

GOODFELLOW SETS OFF FOR THE SUN

The next morning Goodfellow was so excited about his journey to the sun that he couldn't even manage to eat a proper breakfast.

He imagined himself standing before the sun, pleading for his animal friends.

January **1**

GOODFELLOW THE SHEPHERD

In a little cottage on the very edge of a mountain, there lived a shepherd. He had a long name but he was known as Goodfellow because he had never as much as hurt a fly in all his life, and he was always willing to help anyone who needed it.

One cold winter's morning there was a knocking at his door. Goodfellow opened it and saw a little crow with a woollen headscarf wrapped about her ears.

'Klark, klark,' croaked the crow, her voice hoarse with a cold. 'You must help us. There's snow everywhere and not a scrap of food in field or forest. You must go and ask the sun to shine or we animals shall all die of cold and hunger.' 'Me? Go to the sun?' the startled shepherd gasped. 'Don't worry. The magic flying hedgehog will take you,' croaked the crow. 'Tomorrow morning.'

He was so sorry for them that tears began to trickle down his cheeks.

'Don't be silly,' he told himself. 'It's no use crying.'

Suddenly he thought that he ought to take the sun a present. 'What should I take?' he thought. 'What would he really like to receive as a gift?'

Goodfellow looked around his parlour, but he couldn't think of anything. Then his eyes fell on something and he smiled. The alarm clock! He took it down from the shelf, set it to ring just before eight, and went off with it to meet the flying hedgehog.

January 3

THE HEDGEHOG TAKES GOODFELLOW
TO THE SUN

Goodfellow looked at the hedgehog and wondered how he could sit on it. Then he parted the spines on the hedgehog's back, smoothed them down, and sat a-stride the hedgehog as if it were a horse.

'It's like sitting in a tuft of moss,' he said as they flew towards the golden chamber of the sun. They flew over nine mountain ranges and nine forests. Whenever they came to a hill which was especially high or especially steep, the hedgehog rested his magic wings. He rolled himself into a ball around the shepherd and the two rolled down the slope.

Eventually they reached the sun's golden chamber. It was filled with light and ablaze with gold. It took some time for Goodfellow's eyes to grow used to the blinding glare, but when they could see clearly, they saw that the sun was fast asleep.

January 4

IN THE SUN'S GOLDEN CHAMBER

Goodfellow summoned all his courage and said, 'Good morning!'

The sun opened one eyelid, and asked, 'Who are you?'

Goodfellow told the sun his name and why he had come. He told the sun all about how the cruel frost had gripped the mountains around his home. He told him that the snow lay everywhere, that the birds had nothing to eat, the hares and the deer had nothing to nibble at.

'What are you holding?' asked the sun.

'It's a present for you, an alarm clock,' said Goodfellow. 'It will ring before eight.'

'So early?' wondered the sun.

'Is that too early for you?'

'Very well, set it for seven o'clock,' said the sun, 'and I will shine and shine and melt the snow, so that your animal friends will be able to eat and the children can go to school in the light.'

And that's how spring came early to Goodfellow's mountain that year.

January 5

THE WOODSMAN AND THE BEAR

A woodsman went into the forest one day to collect some branches. When he was hungry he lit a fire and took out the sausages that his wife had made for him.

Suddenly there was a great roar as a bear crashed through the undergrowth. When it saw the woodsman, it was about to attack him, but the woodsman held out the sausage for it to eat.

'That was good,' said the bear. 'What was it made off?'

The woodcutter pointed at a wild boar that was creeping through the clearing, trying to avoid being seen by the bear. But the bear saw it and killed it.

'Now make sausages out of it,' it said.

'We'll need to make a fire first,' said the man. He took out his axe and chopped a wedge in a nearby tree. Then he asked the bear to put its paw into the wedge. The silly bear did that and the woodsman went to the other side of the tree and pushed with all his might. The tree began to fall and the bear's paw was trapped in the wedge. The bear couldn't move. The woodsman did not wait to find out what the bear decided to do, and ran home as fast as he could.

January 6

THE THREE KINGS

It had been a hard year for the old lady who lived on the edge of the forest. The snow had fallen and there had been little food for her.

One day in the forest she saw three strangely-dressed men coming towards her. Frightened, she began to run away

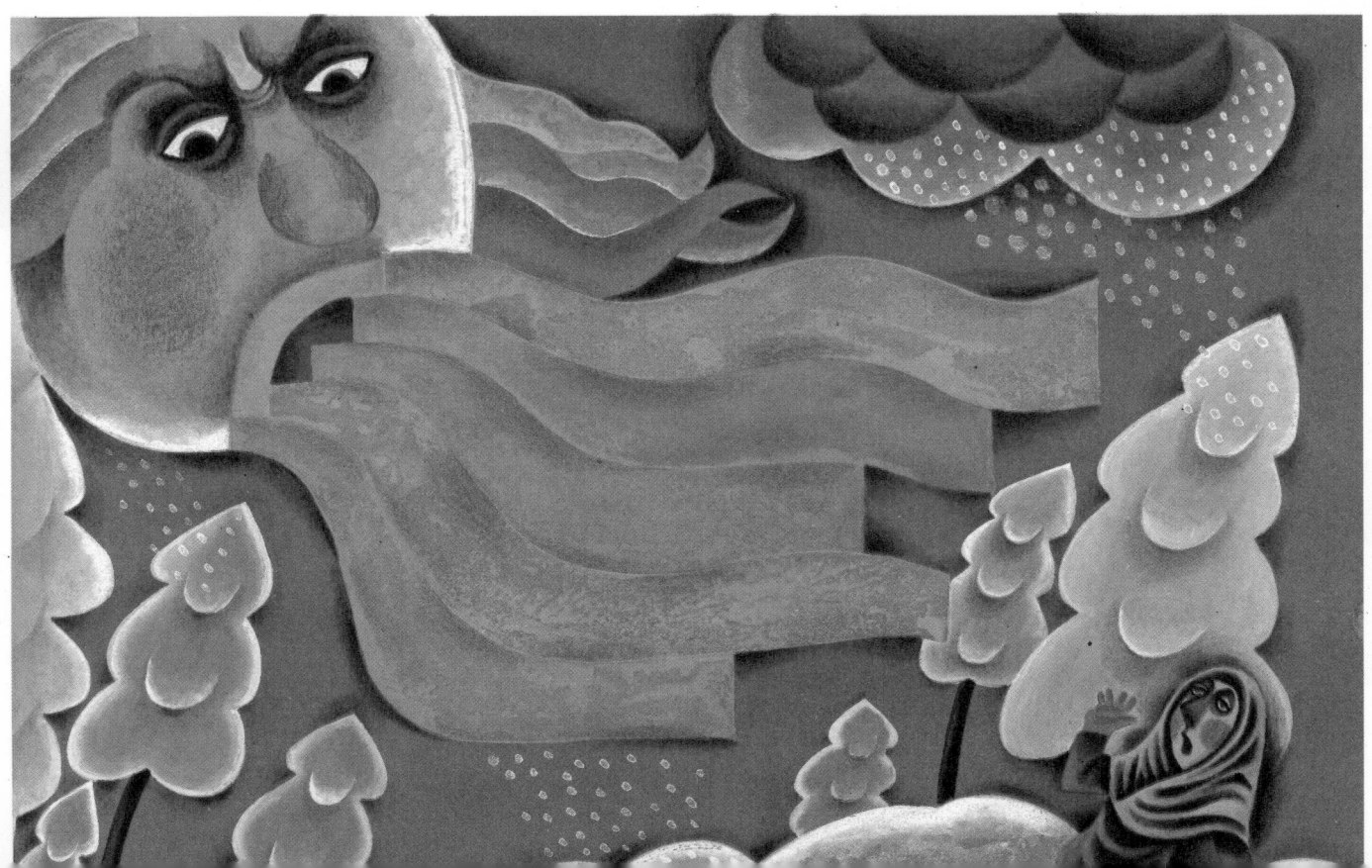

from them, but the three men soon caught up with her and asked her if they could shelter a while in her cottage which they could see nearby.

There, she made them some acorn tea which the three men drank thankfully.

'Where are you off to?' she asked.

'To Bethlehem to see a new-born baby and to give him presents.'

'Why?' asked the old lady.

'Because we believe that he is the Saviour — the son of God. And although we are kings, we will make him our king.'

The three kings opened their bags and gave the old lady some gold, and some precious scents and oils. Before the old lady had time to stammer her thanks, the three kings had gone on their way.

January **7**

JIMMY AND THE SNOWMAN

Jimmy loved the snow. As soon as it had stopped falling he ran into the garden and spent the rest of the day making the

biggest and best snowman you can imagine.

The next morning he was up as early as possible and ran into the garden to look at his snowman. He was horrified when he saw that it was crying.

'What's the matter?' Jimmy asked.

'It's the sun,' said the snowman. 'Its warmth is making me melt. I think I must be dying.'

Poor Jimmy watched as the snowman cried and cried and with each tear that fell it got smaller and smaller and smaller.

But that night it snowed heavily again, so he made another snowman just like the first, but out of the sun's reach, and it lasted until Jimmy went back to school.

January **8**

JIMMY AND THE POLAR BEAR

Jimmy's older sister had given him a wonderful polar bear for his birthday. During the day it never said a word, but in the nighttime when Jimmy and the bear were alone in the bedroom the bear would tell Jimmy about the distant Arctic where all the polar bears lived.

One night the polar bear said to Jimmy, 'You know I've been here for such a long time and you have never given me anything to eat. I'm getting very hungry.'

Jimmy thought and thought: What could he give his polar bear to eat?

Suddenly he had a brainwave. He crept down into the kitchen and opened the refrigerator very quietly so as not to disturb anyone. A few minutes later he was back in the room. What do you think he had with him for the bear to eat? Lovely cold ice cream.

Jimmy and the bear ate it together: a spoonfool for the bear and then one for Jimmy, and so on until the carton was quite empty.

January 9

THE LITTLE CLOUD

Poor little cloud. He wanted to be big so that he could drop raindrops onto the

earth and help the flowers and trees to grow. But all the big clouds laughed at him when he told them this.

'You're far too small,' they all said. 'Go away and don't bother us.'

The cloud drifted away from all the other clouds and floated off on his own. He was so sad that he began to cry and his little teardrops fell down to the earth and landed on a little snowdrop that was just beginning to push its way through the brown soil. It was very grateful to the little cloud for giving it some water, for it had been quite thirsty, and looked up into the sky and smiled at the cloud.

The cloud saw the smile and was very proud. He knew then that one day he would be big enough to help the other rainclouds.

January 10

PETER'S DREAM

One night Peter dreamed that he was in the garden beside the snowdrop and the cloud floated down to say 'Hallo' to them.

'What's it like in the sky?' asked Peter.

'Why don't you come up and see?' said the cloud: so Peter climbed up onto the cloud's back and they floated up and up into the sky above. Peter had a wonderful view of his house looking very small.

'I can' t support you any longer,' cried the cloud suddenly.

Peter was very scared as he felt himself slip through the cloud and fall down to the ground below. Down and down he tumbled; down and down. All of a sudden he landed with a heavy thud. He woke up with a start and what do you think had happened? He had fallen right out of his bed and was lying on the floor beside it.

January 11

PETER AND THE SNOWDROP

The next night Peter dreamed that the snowdrop came to him, only it had changed into a beautiful princess.

'You must help us,' pleaded the snowdrop princess. 'The wicked weeds have started to grow and are choking us to death.'

'What can I do?' asked Peter.

'You must dig them up and throw them away. Please Peter.'

The next morning Peter dressed quickly and ran down to the snowdrop. The snowdrop princess had been right. There were several snowdrops coming through, but some early weeds were choking them to death.

Peter ran and got a hoe from the garden shed. He was soon busy hoeing away and did not stop until every weed had been pulled up.

'Whatever's happened to Peter?' asked his father.

'I don't know,' said Peter's mother. 'Perhaps he hurt his head when he fell out of bed the night before last.'

January 12

THE UNGRATEFUL CHICKEN

Once upon a time there was a poor old man and woman who were very happy. Their most prized possession was a black hen and one day they were very surprised when she laid a large egg.

Eventually the big egg hatched and the biggest chicken that the old couple had ever seen popped out. They gave it some corn which the chicken ate hungrily and still it pecked around for more. The more it ate the bigger it became.

The old man could stand it no longer, so he got his axe out and cut the chicken's head off. His wife then plucked it and cooked it, but it was so big that they could not possibly eat it all themselves.

So they cut the cooked chicken into small pieces and sold them to their neighbours and soon had enough money to buy all the food they could eat.

January 13

THE EXOTIC BIRD

When Uncle Charles was feeding the birds, he liked to let them peck titbits straight from his hand. If he went for a walk in the park, he would fill a coconut shell with grains of poppy seed, millet or bird-seed. When he got to the park he would put some grains into the palm of his hand, and it would take an hour or two before the coconut shell was empty.

One day, he was holding out a titbit for his bird friends when there was a whirring of wings, and there on his hand appeared a strange bird.

'You're not from round here, are you?' he asked.

'Dear me, no,' the bird replied.

'From somewhere in the tropics?' asked Uncle Charles.

'No. From the snow-covered woods up above the town,' twittered the bird. 'But no one ever feeds us there.'

From then on, during wintertime, Uncle Charles began to feed the birds in the woods as well as those in the park.

January 14

GRANNY'S SPINNING WHEEL

Phillip's Granny was a strange little old lady. She spent most of her time sitting by her spinning wheel making wool, out of fleece. Phillip used to watch the wheel for hour after hour, his eyes gleaming as the wheel went round and round and round.

One day the old lady said, 'Would you like to learn how to spin?'

'Oh yes, please,' cried Phil excitedly.

So the old woman sat Phillip on her knee and taught him how to feed the carded fleece through the spindle and make the woollen yarn. After quite a long time there was enough wool for Phillip's mother to knit him a lovely sweater.

You can imagine how proud Phillip was when he wore the sweater to school for the first time. All his classmates were quite envious when he told them that he had actually made the wool which his mother had knitted.

THE GINGERBREAD HOUSE

Jack and Jenny lived in a little cottage with their parents. One day they went into the forest to gather some mushrooms.

They wandered deeper and deeper into the forest until they saw a house made of gingerbread and marzipan.

The two children were quite hungry so they fell on the house and began to eat it.

'WHAT DO YOU THINK YOU'RE DOING?' shouted a voice.

The children looked down and saw an old witch.

'It's just like the witch in that story Daddy read to us, Jack,' said Jenny.

The two children ran as fast as their legs could carry them and after a few hundred yards bumped into their father, who had been so worried that he had come to look for them.

'Daddy,' cried Jenny. 'We've just escaped from a wicked witch.'

'Well then,' said Daddy. 'I think that we'd better get away from here as fast as we can.' And that's just what they did.

January 16

THE FOX AND THE STORK

The fox and the stork were great friends. One day the fox invited the stork to come and eat with him. When the stork arrived the fox spooned some runny porridge onto a large plate. Before the stork had time to take a peck at the food, the fox had gobbled it all up.

The stork decided to pay the fox back. He cooked some lovely chicken, which he knew the fox liked, put them in a long-necked bottle and asked his friend the fox to share his feast with him.

'Help yourself, Fox, help yourself,' said the stork. But the bottle had such a narrow neck that the fox could not reach inside.

The stork put his long beak into the bottle and ate as much as he could. 'Don't you like chicken, Fox?' he asked.

'Yes, but I can't get at it,' replied the fox.

'If you promise not to be so greedy again, I'll ask you to eat with me tomorrow,' said the stork.

So the fox promised and since then they have often had lovely meals together with each eating his fill.

January 17

THE PLAGUE OF MICE

There was once a kingdom that was overrun with mice. Even the king's throne room was crowded with mice.

Things got so bad that the king issued a proclamation that whoever managed

to rid the country of the mice should receive half his kingdom.

Now it happened that two little boys heard the proclamation and ran to tell their grandmother about it. The old lady was really a witch, but she was a good witch so she gave the boys a magic trumpet, and said, 'Give this to the princess and tell her to blow it with all her might.'

They did as she bid, went to the palace and gave the trumpet to the king's daughter. She blew with all her might. Not a sound came out.

The old king cupped his hand to his ear and said, 'Can't hear a thing, blow harder, child.'

The princess blew even harder but still not a sound came out. But the mice heard something. Notes so soft that human ears could not pick them up. All of a sudden the mice stopped scurrying hither and thither and left the palace, and the palace mice led the town mice out of the kingdom for ever.

The grateful king gave the two boys half his kingdom as he had promised.

January 18

THE ANIMALS AND THE ROBBERS

One day, a billy-goat, a cockerel, a cat and a dog decided to set off on their travels. Just as it was getting dark, they discovered a cottage in the forest. They decided that this would be a pleasant place to live, but when the goat peeped in through the window there were four big men sitting round the table.

'They are robbers!' whispered the billy-goat.

'What are they doing?' asked the cat.

'Playing cards,' replied the goat.

The animals gathered round to decide what they should do. First the goat stuck his horns through the window-pane.

'A devil!' screamed the robbers.

Then the cockerel flew in the window, blew out the lamp, and, crowing loudly, knocked off the robbers' hats.

The robbers were so frightened that they ran away and never came back again. The animals made their home there, each in his usual place: the dog in the yard, the goat in the scullery, the cockerel on his perch and the cat on the stove. And they all lived happily together for many years.

January 19

WHY DOGS GROWL AT CATS

Long ago dogs became man's best friends and the king of all the dogs was given a parchment saying this. The king dog gave the parchment to his chamberlain, who put it in a cupboard for safety.

Now the cats were very jealous of this and one night they stole the parchment.

One day the dogs decided that they wanted to have a look at the parchment and sent the chamberlain to get it. Imagine his surprise when the document was not there. All that was there was a cat's whisker. The king dog immediately ordered the leader of the cats to come before him and threatened him with all sorts of punishment if the document was not returned. The scared cat went to where the parchment had been hidden and was horrified to find it was not there. All that there was was a mouse's whisker. He ordered that the chief mouse be brought before him and the mouse confessed that they had eaten it.

The cat reported this to the dogs who were furious and growled angrily at the cat. The cat ran out of the room and went to chase the mouse to punish him. Things haven't changed to this day.

IDLE JACK

Jack was the laziest boy in the village. All he did every day was lie by the stove, sleeping. He only woke up to eat the meals that his poor mother cooked for him. Then he would go back to sleep again.

His mother became angrier and angrier and one day she woke him up roughly and told him to get out of her house. All she gave him was some currant buns.

Poor Jack. He decided to go to the royal city to seek his fortune. On his way he met an old lady who looked very hungry, so he gave her some of the buns. The old woman was very grateful and gave Jack some magic powder. She told him that whatever he sprinkled it on would grow ten times larger.

Jack set on his way and arrived at the royal city and asked to be directed to the royal palace.

January 21

AT THE PALACE

When Jack arrived in the king's chamber he saw the poor, thin king comforting his poor, thin daughter.

'Is there nothing to eat?' asked Jack.

'Nothing at all,' said the king. 'A plague of rats came to the town and they ate everything. And when they had done that they went off.'

'Did they leave nothing?'

'Only one miserable chicken and one corn seed. But what good are they?'

'Bring them to me,' said Jack.

The surprised monarch did as Jack had said and when the chicken and the seed were before him, Jack took some of the magic powder from his tunic and sprinkled it over the bird and the grain. Suddenly there were ten chickens and ten seeds. Jack then sprinkled some more magic powder over each chicken and he continued until all the powder had been used up and there were thousands of squawking chickens and sacks and sacks of grain. The famine was over. The king was as good as his word and the princess and Jack were married that very day.

January 22

THE BLACKSMITH AND THE KNIGHT

One day a knight came riding by and asked a poor 'smith to make him one thousand horseshoes.

When the knight returned he was very pleased with the 'smith's work and loaded the shoes onto a cart behind his horse.

'Money!' scoffed the knight, when the 'smith asked him for payment. 'Bah!' and he threw some horse dung at the poor 'smith.

Now all this had been seen by an old witch who took pity on the blacksmith.

She immediately cast two spells.

The knight was riding off when suddenly his horse shied up and he was thrown off the animal's back and was killed.

The 'smith did not see this happen. He picked up the dung and threw it at a tree nearby. Immediately the tree split open and a shower of golden coins fell to the earth.

With all the money the 'smith built a splendid new house where he lived happily ever after.

January 23

LITTLE RED RIDING HOOD

Once upon a time a little girl called Little Red Riding Hood went to visit her grandmother, who lived at the other side of the forest.

Half-way there she met a wolf who asked her where she was going. When she told him, the wolf ran ahead and arrived at grandmother's house before Little Red Riding Hood. He ran into her parlour and before you could say 'Jack Flash', the wolf gobbled the old lady up. He ran into her bedroom and put on her nightgown and nightcap.

A few seconds later Little Red Riding Hood came in. 'What big eyes you have, Grandmama,' she said.

'All the better to see you with, my dear,' said the wolf.

'What big ears you have, Grandmama,' the girl said.

'All the better to hear you with, my dear,' came the reply.

'What big teeth you have, Grandmama,' said the girl.

'All the better to eat you with,' and as he said the words the wolf jumped out of bed and grabbed the terrified girl.

She looked at him with large, tearful eyes and said in a soft voice, 'I know that you are a wolf and that it is in your nature to eat people. I forgive you.' And so saying she kissed the wolf on his ghastly mouth. Immediately he turned into the handsomest prince and said, 'Thank you. You have freed me from a spell that a wicked witch put on me a long time ago.'

As soon as Red Riding Hood had released the prince from the spell, the poor old grandmother magically reappeared and lived happily ever after.

January 24

THE BOOK IMP

One day a little boy called Timmy was curled up reading a book when an imp appeared.

'Who are you?' asked Timmy, quite astonished.

'I'm the book imp,' said the little fellow. 'Once I was just like you, I read and read and read and did nothing else. I never went out to play and I never made any friends. And one day I became smaller and smaller and smaller and

became so small that I could live in the spine of this book!'

All of a sudden Timmy woke up, for he had been dreaming, but from then on he went out more often and made lots of friends.

January 25

THE BOOK IMP AGAIN

A few days later Timmy and one of his new friends picked up the book and Timmy began to read his friend a story.

All of a sudden Timmy heard a bell jangle and he was astonished to see the book imp appear.

'I'd thought I'd dreamed you,' said Timmy.

'I know,' said the book imp. 'I made you have that dream. Always remember, Timmy, books can be very good friends, but they can never be as real as proper people. I'm glad that you've made friends.'

And having said that the book imp disappeared for ever.

January 26

THE HORSE AND THE OX

One day two farmers came to market. One was rich and the other was as poor as a church mouse. The rich man rode a fine horse and the poor man sat astride an old oxen. They both sold what they had to sell and bought what they needed.

The rich man had to purchase some foul-smelling mothballs and some strong-smelling cheese, and the poor man, because it was his wife's birthday, had bought her some sweet-smelling soap.

The proud thoroughbred horse was horrified when he smelt his load. It was, he felt, below his dignity to carry it, so he bolted and ran off.

'Never mind,' said the poor man. 'My ox is strong enough to carry your things and mine.' And he loaded the cheese and mothballs onto his ox.

The rich man was so impressed with the poor man's generosity that he gave him a purse of gold.

'Nonsense,' said Alice. 'That's the train I always take.'

'That one's broken down,' replied the guard.

'Rubbish!' said Alice and went and sat in the train.

A few moments later another train came in, stopped for a moment and then, when no one got on, drew slowly out of the station. Alice watched smugly from her train, and then gasped in horror, for she knew some of the passengers on it. The guard *had* told her the truth. That taught her a lesson; didn't it?

January **27**

ALICE AND THE STATION MASTER

Once a month Alice went by train to visit her father, who lived in another town away from Alice and her mother.

One day when she arrived at the station the guard who knew her well said, 'It's a different train you're getting today, Alice.'

January **28**

THE PIGEON AND THE SQUIRREL

All autumn long the squirrel had been busy gathering nuts to make sure that they had enough food for the winter. None of the other animals bothered to help, but when winter came they found that there was not enough food for them all to eat.

The pigeon, who had been elected leader, flew to the squirrel's drey and wakened him up. 'We need some of your store of nuts or else we will starve, for there is no food for us to eat.'

'Tough!' retorted the squirrel. 'I worked hard all autumn while you all played. Now go away, I'm going back to sleep.'

'If we all promise to help you next autumn, will you give us some nuts now?' asked the pigeon.

The squirrel replied, 'I suppose so, if you promise solemnly.' The pigeon did as he was asked and the squirrel told him to help himself to all the nuts the animals needed.

The next year all the animals helped the squirrel collect nuts and they all had plenty to eat the whole winter through.

January **29**

THE MAGIC HAND-MILL

Two brothers lived in the same village. One was a rich farmer, the other a poor labourer. One day, the rich man slaughtered a pig and his brother came to ask for some meat.

'Rather than give you anything,' said the rich man, angrily, 'I should send a hamper to the devil in hell!'

The brother scathingly said that he would take it for him and set off for hell. Suddenly he realized he had got lost. 'Where am I?' he said.

'Why, in hell of course,' replied the devil who had appeared from nowhere.

And in exchange for the pork he gave the poor man an old hand-mill.

When the poor man took the hand-mill home, he found that it ground him food, drink and money. And since he was no miser, the rest of the village wanted for nothing ever again.

January **30**

THE STOLEN HONEY

One day a hunter was going through the woods when all of a sudden he came across a large bear, looking very upset.

'What's wrong, bear?' asked the hunter.

'During the night someone has stolen my honey. What shall I do?'

'Let's follow the trail and see where it leads us,' said the hunter.

The bear agreed and the honey trail

led them right into the fox's lair.

'Foxy,' cried the hunter. 'Can we see you a minute?'

'I want my honey,' growled the bear.

'What honey?' asked the fox, licking his lips as he spoke.

'The honey you stole from me last night. It was in a big barrel.'

'Nonsense!' cried the fox. 'Why should I steal your honey?'

Just then a little voice shouted from inside, 'Daddy. Silly baby's knocked over the bear's honey pot and it's running all over the place.'

The fox ran inside and reappeared a few seconds later with the honey pot. 'Just my little joke,' he said quietly.

The bear punched the fox on the eye and it immediately began to swell. 'Just my little joke,' said the bear and picked up his barrel and walked off.

January **31**

BIG, BROAD AND EAGLE-EYE

Once upon a time a wicked wizard kidnapped a beautiful princess. The king called for his three advisors, Big, Broad and Eagle-Eye.

'The wizard will only release my daughter if I can get him one of the dawn pearls that lie at the bottom of the sea.'

'Leave it to us,' said Eagle-Eye. 'We will get one for you.'

The three men set out to the ocean edge. Eagle-Eye, who was the sharpest-sighted man in the world, looked into the deep sea and saw right at the bottom a shining dawn pearl.

Big, who had the longest arms in the

world, rowed out to sea and when he was over the pearl, he simply leaned over the side and picked the dawn pearl off the sea bed.

The three then set out for the wizard's castle and when they showed the wizard the dawn pearl he handed the princess over.

Now, unfortunately, just as they were about to leave, Eagle-Eye was so busy looking at something in the distance that he didn't see a boulder and tripped over it, breaking his ankle.

But it didn't really matter, for Broad, who was feeling a little guilty at not having done anything to help the princess escape, simply picked up his two friends and the princess and carried them home.

February 1

THE SHEPHERD AND THE WOLVES

A shepherd was once threatened by wolves that said they would kill him unless he told them where the sheep were hidden.

'All right,' said the shepherd, 'I'll tell you. They are in the field that's exactly so many wolves' paces from here.'

'How many?' asked the wolves.

'Two score less half a dozen plus a half score times a dozen and a half.'

'How many?' asked the wolf again.

'Two score less half a dozen plus a half score times a dozen and a half. Now if you will excuse me while you're working that out, I must go.'

The wolves were far too busy puzzling over the distance so they did not follow the shepherd. Perhaps the wolves are still counting, who knows?

February 2

THE WOLF AND THE FOX

One day in the forest, a wolf met a fox. 'I haven't eaten for three days,' said the wolf. 'I am so hungry.'

'You've only got yourself to blame,' said the fox. 'I always have plenty to eat. Yesterday I had some lovely plump duck.'

'Where did you get that?' asked the wolf.

'I laid down in the path and pretended to be dead. A farmer stopped and said to his wife, "That's a fine tail on the fox," picked me up and threw me into his cart, which was full of ducks. I picked the plumpest and was off before you could say "Jack Robinson".'

A few hours later the wolf was waiting by the roadside when he heard the trundle of cartwheels. He immediately laid in the road pretending to be dead. But it

was the same farmer who the fox had fooled and he picked up his shotgun and peppered the wolf with shot.

The wolf ran off and never talked to the fox again.

February 3

THE MAGIC UMBRELLAS

It was sleeting very heavily and Mat and Peg were bored with being indoors. They asked if they could go outside.

'I suppose so,' their mother said. 'But take your umbrellas.'

'Why are they called "umbrellas", Mummy?' asked Mat.

'A long time ago ladies used to hate getting sun in their faces. White skins were thought to be much more attractive than tanned ones. But it was too hot in some countries to stay indoors, so someone invented a collapsible shade that could be carried around and put up when the sun shone too strongly.'

'But why are they called "umbrellas"?' asked Peg.

'From two old words. One was "umbra", which meant shade, and the other was "elle", which meant lady. So "umbrella" used to mean shade for the lady,' said Mummy.

'Let's go out now,' said Mat.

'OK,' said Peg, 'but I'm going to keep my umbrella up when the sleet stops and the sun shines. I'm going to keep my skin pure and white.'

THE GREEN DWARF AND THE CAT

What *is* the green dwarf doing up the tree? Well, it was one of those days in February when Spring seems to have come early, so the green dwarf had decided to go for a walk.

As he walked through the woods he heard, all of a sudden, a cat mewing up above him. He looked up and saw a lovely little kitten stuck in the tree. Quick as a flash he climbed the tree to rescue the kitten, but as soon as he reached the top, the kitten jumped down safely, leaving the green dwarf stuck. He had not realized how tall the tree was and when he looked down he felt dizzy.

'Help!' he cried, and fortunately

February **4**

THE GREEN DWARF

In a quiet pool, deep in the cool water there lived a little green dwarf. He was really very happy there.

In the winter, however, there was one thing that really worried him. When it became very cold the water above him would freeze over and he had to make sure that the ice did not spread above the roof of his cottage.

As soon as it started to freeze, he would grab his axe and chop all the ice away. Sometimes he had to do this several times a day.

One night he dreamed that the ice had frozen over so thickly that he could not chop it away. He became colder and colder until at last he thought that he surely must die. All of a sudden he woke up and it was not surprising that he was so cold. He had been chopping so hard in his sleep that all the blankets had come off the bed. He tucked them around him again and went back to sleep.

a friendly sparrow who was flying past landed on the branch beside him and the little green dwarf climbed onto its back and was carried down to the ground below.

THE CRAYFISH BARBER

One day the little green dwarf went to the barber who happened to be a crayfish. 'Short back and sides?' asked the fish when the little green dwarf was sitting in his chair.

The dwarf nodded and the crayfish set to work. It was very slow and the little green dwarf nodded off to sleep.

'I'm sorry,' said the crayfish, when the dwarf wakened up, 'but as you slept I thought I'd trim your moustache a little. I took a bit off one side, but I took too much off the other. And then I took too much off the first side to try to balance it and . . . on it went until there was no moustache left.'

I wonder if it will grow again!

FISH TO THE RESCUE

The little green dwarf was sitting in a very odd position. His arms were straight out in front of him. And when he moved one forward, the other moved backward of its own accord.

Fortunately for him a perch swam by and saw his problem.

'If I can cure you what will you give me?' it asked.

'What would you like?' asked the dwarf, struggling away.

'Two weeks supply of ants' eggs, my favourite food.'

'Very well,' he said.

The perch swam round in front of the dwarf and took his coat off. Immediately the dwarf could move his arms again.

The clever fish had spotted that the dwarf had left the coathanger in his coat. No wonder he couldn't move his arms.

February **8**

THE CARPENTER AND THE FAIRY

In a village there lived a hard-working and skilful carpenter. After some time he had made furniture for every house in the village and, as there was no more work, he set out to find work elsewhere.

One evening, he arrived in a deep forest. He looked around for the softest patch of moss on which to sleep for the night. Suddenly, there in front of him stood a fairy, and a dozen sprites. The fairy made a sign to them and out of their bundles they took planes and saws. In a few minutes the carpenter found himself standing in front of a bed, a table and a chair which were carved so perfectly that it did not seem possible.

The carpenter's weariness left him, and he examined the furniture closely. That night he returned to his village, and began to make tables, chairs and beds just like the ones the fairies had made. The villagers gasped when they saw how beautiful the furniture was, and they began to order new tables and chairs, which kept the carpenter busy until he decided to retire.

February **9**

THE TWO FROGS

Two frogs once jumped up onto a lily pad and announced that they were the greatest doctors in the world. They could, they claimed, cure any animal of any disease, and also make them better looking.

All the other animals gathered round to listen to them, and then the jackal said, 'How dare you claim that, why don't you mend your legs so that you can walk properly?'

'And why don't you do something about your skin?' asked a sheep.

'And your eyes are all bulgy and ugly,' shouted an ox.

'But we are meant to look like this,' cried one of the frogs.

'And we are meant to look like this,' cried the jackal, the sheep and the ox.

When they heard the animals' words the two frogs realized that perhaps they should have thought of that before they made their announcement and hopped back into the pond and stayed there.

February 10

THE GREEN DWARF'S TRUMPET

The green dwarf was so excited. He had been invited to a fancy dress party and he had made himself a splendid cape and a wonderful hat with a feather on it.

His friend the perch had made him a wooden sword and off he set dressed up as one of the Three Musketeers.

Imagine how upset he was when he arrived at the party and found not just one, but three of his friends had had the same idea.

'Never mind,' said someone. 'Here's a trumpet. Why don't you pretend that you are not a musketeer, but a town crier. You can make announcements and when you blow your trumpet everyone will stop and listen to you.'

The little dwarf did just that and had a fabulous time blowing his own trumpet and announcing the games that were to be played. And when tea was ready he gave an especially loud fanfare.

February 11

MORE ABOUT THE GREEN DWARF'S TRUMPET

Everyone who had been at the party had enjoyed the little green man's trumpeting so much that they talked about it for many days after.

News even reached the ears of the King and Queen and a few days later the

little green man was astonished to receive a command to appear before the monarch at a very important ball. He dressed himself up in his cloak and feathered hat and made his way to the royal palace.

The King told him that each time a dance was to begin, he should blow his trumpet and announce the dance.

The little green dwarf was so proud as he did as he was commanded, and especially pleased when the Princess herself asked if he would dance with her.

When he got home all his friends listened with amazement when he told them all about his night at the royal ball.

February 12

PICKING THE BERRIES

Simon and Suzie went into the woods one day to pick berries for their mother, who was going to make jam. They had a wonderful time reaching high into the bushes where the plumpest berries were and gradually their bowl became full.

As they made their way home, Simon decided to have just one berry, so Suzie decided to have one too; and then Simon decided to have one more and Suzie had another one... When they got home Mummy smiled when she saw the empty bowl and the juice marks around the childrens' mouths.

'It's just as well I already made some jam,' she said. 'Would you like some for tea?'

'Not today,' said Simon. 'I've had enough already.'

And Suzie agreed with him.

February 13

GUY'S BIG ADVENTURE

Guy was a little boy who never listened to what his mother told him. One day

she said, 'Don't go out today, Guy. I've just heard that the Magic Stag has escaped from the zoo.'

As usual, Guy disobeyed his mother and as soon as her back was turned, he went out to play. Well, of course, he had not gone more than a few yards when he heard the sound of the Magic Stag's hooves on the road. Guy tried to hide but it was no good, the Magic Stag picked him up and placed him on his back. Before the frightened boy could do anything, the stag was off — over hill and dale the stag ran and Guy had to hang on for his life.

'Where are you taking me?' he cried.

'To a place where you will never be able to disobey your mother again.'

'Oh please take me home, I promise

never to disobey Mummy again,' cried Guy.

'Do you really promise?'

'Yes!' promised Guy.

So the Magic Stag carried Guy home and he always kept his promise.

Do you think that Guy had been dreaming?

February **14**

THE TWO WATER NYMPHS

Once upon a time there were two nymphs who lived in a glade in the countryside. There were other nymphs who lived with them, but these two nymphs never did a stroke of work. Instead all day and every day they would rise from their beds and dance until bedtime.

The other nymphs used to try to make them help them at their labours but it was no use, the two nymphs danced and danced and danced.

When winter came the hard-working nymphs had laid aside plenty of food to make sure thay had enough to last them through the ice-cold months. The two dancing nymphs had nothing to eat.

They went to their sister nymphs and asked for some food, but the others refused. 'You could have been wise and stored up for winter.'

The two nymphs became thinner and thinner and eventually died.

You see, it's all right to play some of the time, but you must always remember to plan ahead as best you can.

February 15

THE POOR MAN WHO BECAME KING

A poor miller's son was making his way to town one day when he came across an ant, an eagle and a lion squabbling over a round cheese. The lad took out his knife and cut the cheese into three equal pieces. He gave an equal part to each animal. In return the ant gave him one of its legs, the eagle one of its feathers and the lion gave him three hairs. They told him how to use them.

The lad thanked them all and continued his journey. When he arrived at the town he heard that an ogre had carried off the young queen and that whoever could free her from its clutches should marry her and become king.

The poor lad remembered the presents that the animals had given him. He placed the ant's leg in his mouth and immediately became tiny. He held the eagle's feather in his hand and could immediately fly off to the ogre's castle. When he arrived there he put the lion's hairs under his arm and immediately became as strong as three lions. With this strength he was able to free the queen.

The queen fell in love with her saviour. As soon as they were married he became king and ruled well and wisely for many years.

February 16

HOW A COW MADE TWO BUTCHERS INTO FARMERS

Two butchers bought a cow from a farmer and were taking it home for slaughter when the cow said to them, 'Why kill me, let me live and I will give you much creamy milk every day.'

The two butchers agreed and every day from then on the cow gave them rich creamy milk. There was too much for the butchers to drink on their own, so they sold the extra milk.

It was so good that people came from far and near to buy it and the butchers became quite rich and decided to buy another cow. This gave just as rich and creamy milk as the first and made them enough money to buy a third, then a fourth and soon a whole herd of cows.

They soon had so many cows that they had to buy lots of land to keep them and they became so interested in rearing cattle that they gave up their butchers' business and became full-time farmers.

February 17

THE GARDENER AND THE DOG

The gardener was drawing water from the well one day. He was planning to use it to water some seeds that he had just planted. His little dog was playing at the well and unfortunately fell in.

Without thinking the gardener took

his clothes off and climbed down into the well to rescue it. Just as he was nearing the top with the dog under his arm, the frightened dog bit his hand.

'You ungrateful wretch,' exclaimed the gardener. 'I feed you and risk my own life to rescue you. You can jolly well pull yourself out.' And with that he dropped the dog back in the well.

You may think that that was a very cruel thing to do—but there is a moral to this story—never bite the hand that feeds you!

February 18

THE BIRD THAT TRIED TO ESCAPE

There was once a little bird who got very bored flying around in its cage all day. How it longed to be able to fly free, through the air. He little realized that he would not be able to survive outside, for the winter was very cold and he came from a warm country.

One day little Pamela, who owned the bird, forgot to lock its cage door properly, and seizing its chance, the little bird flew out of the cage and into the room. It had a marvellous time flying around.

'Get back into your cage,' shouted the vacuum cleaner which happened to be in the room at the time. 'It's dangerous for you out of your cage.'

But the little bird ignored the cleaner and made to fly into the garden outside.

Just as the bird was about to escape, the vacuum cleaner switched itself on and sucked the bird back into the room.

Pamela heard the noise and ran into the room where she found the bird out of its cage.

She immediately put it back and switched off the cleaner, never once suspecting that the old cleaner had saved her bird's life.

February 19

THE FUNNY FLAG

There was once a king who had everything he wanted which made it very difficult for his wife to buy him birthday presents. He had a crown, so she could not buy him that. He had splendid robes, so she could not buy him those. And he had a lovely sword, so she could not buy him that. What could she buy him?

One year she had a terrific idea. Every night after the king had gone to bed she sewed and sewed and sewed and on the day of his birthday she gave the king the beautiful cloth that she had stitched.

'What is it?' he asked her in a very surprised voice.

'It's an idea I had,' said the Queen. 'The two swords represent your authority and the plumed helmet your prowess

31

in battle. And the deep colour represents my deep love for you.'

The king was so happy with his wife's present that he tied it to a staff and flew it like a flag so that everyone could see how powerful he was and how much his wife loved him.

two sons began to dig deep in the vineyard believing that their father had buried treasure there. They turned over the soil again and again but found nothing.

'Now that we have done all this digging we may as well plant some new vines.'

This they did and because they had dug so deep the vines flourished and produced a finer vintage than before.

You see the old man had known that the two sons were basically lazy and would not dig the vineyard unless they believed there would be a reward.

And there was a reward, wasn't there? Maybe not the one that the two lads suspected, but one that made them just as rich.

February 20

THE FARMER AND HIS SONS

A farmer was once close to death and he called his two sons to him and said, 'My sons, I am now almost ready to die and all I have to leave you is buried in the vineyard.'

As soon as the old man was dead, the

February 21

THE MICE IN THE SACK

Some mice once set up home in the loft of a farmer's barn. They made their house next to a pile of wheat so that they would have plenty to eat close at hand.

Sometimes, of course, the farmer came in with his shovel and put some of

the wheat into sacks. The pile of wheat gradually became smaller and smaller and smaller until the little mice became very worried indeed.

One day the farmer came in with his shovel and scooped up the last of the wheat, taking the mice and their house with it. The poor mice were very scared when they realized what was happening, but there was little they could do.

I wonder how they got out. Perhaps we'll find out later.

February **22**

THE MILLER AND HIS CAT

The little mice were carried by cart to the miller who bought the wheat from the farmer. He carried it into his mill and as it was very late he went to bed as soon as it was stored.

A few minutes later he was sound asleep. He was very angry, indeed, when his cat wakened him up a few hours later and pointed his paw towards the loft.

'What is it, Puss?' he asked.

The cat continued pointing toward the loft, mewing all the time. The miller

got out of bed and went to the loft where he was astonished to see something inside the sack that the farmer had sold him.

'It must be magic,' mewed the terrified cat.

'We'll soon find out,' said the miller. 'Stay here, cat, I'll go and get my gun.'

The poor mice inside the sack were

shaking with terror. I wonder if they managed to escape.

February **23**

HOW THE MICE ESCAPED

When the miller was looking for his gun the mice began to shake with terror and the cat was so sure that there was something magical about the sack that he ran off to hide.

Hearing nothing outside, the mice began to gnaw through the canvas sack. Just in time, they made their way out as the miller came back with his gun. He fired two shots into the sack and as nothing moved, he decided that there was nothing wrong with the sack after all. He called the cat and the two left the loft and went to bed.

The mice saw what had happened from their hiding place. They thought that it would be safer to leave the loft when suddenly one of them realized that they were in a flour mill. The mice screeched with delight because flour mills are where mice like best of all to be.

They decided to live there but to be very careful to keep out of everyone's way.

I wonder if they are still there.

February 24

THE FATHER AND HIS DAUGHTERS

A man who had two daughters allowed one to marry a gardener and the other a potter. After the wedding the two girls went off with their husbands and left the father alone.

The next spring the father went to visit the daughter who had married the

gardener. 'We are very happy, Father,' said the girl, 'but we would be happier if only it would rain. We need rain to water our plants.'

Later the same day, the father visited the daughter who had married the potter. 'We are very happy, Father,' said the girl. 'And we will stay happy as long as the sun shines so hotly as today, for then our tiles bake so quickly.'

'How unfortunate that I cannot pray for the weather that both you and your sister wish. She wants rain, you want sunshine.'

'Never mind, Father,' said the girl. 'It is impossible to please everyone all of the time.'

How impressed the man was at his daughter's wisdom.

February 25

FREDERICK MOVES HOUSE

Frederick was a poor orphan boy who decided to move house. He packed all his belongings onto a barrow and began to push it through the woods. 'Where are you going?' asked the robin. 'I don't know, but I am bored living here and have decided to leave.' 'What did he say?' asked the rabbit. 'He said he's bored living here and he's moving away,' said the robin. 'Why? We'll miss him dreadfully if he goes,' said the rabbit. 'Can't we make him stay?' Now Frederick had no idea that his friends would miss him so. He stopped pushing and thought for a moment. 'If I stay, will you help me paint my house and dig my garden?' he asked. 'Oh yes. We'll do

The lad went back to the cooper's shop and told the cooper this.

'There must be someone who will marry me. Go out again, boy.'

The lad did as he was asked but the same thing happened again.

'Well, if that's their attitude,' said the cooper, 'they can jolly well stay unmarried for all I care. And I will, too.'

Remember, if a job's worth doing, it's worth doing yourself.

anything if you stay. And so will all the other animals.' So Frederick went home and lived happily with his animal friends for many years.

February 27

THE COOPER TAKES A WIFE

The cooper had been working so hard

February 26

THE COOPER OF FIFE

Once upon a time in a part of Scotland — called Fife — there was a cooper. Coopers spend all their time making barrels and don't have much time for anything else. This cooper spent so much time at his work that he was quite old before he realized that he had not taken a wife. He called his assistant and said to him, 'I have no time to find a wife. Go out and find one for me.'

The lad went out into the town and asked many unmarried women if they would marry the cooper. They all said the same thing. 'If the cooper wants to marry me, he can jolly well ask me himself.'

that one day he fell asleep at his work. He had an awful dream that he was old and lonely and had no one to care for him.

When he woke up he ran to his home and put his best clothes on. He picked some flowers from his garden and went to call on the lady next door whom he had always liked a great deal.

He asked her if she would marry him.

'Of course I will,' she said. 'I've been waiting for ages for you to ask me.'

So the cooper was married and the two lived happily ever after.

THE SHY PRINCESS

Once upon a time there was an old queen who wanted to retire and give her kingdom to her only daughter, Princess Helena.

But the princess was so shy she would not go out of the palace to meet the people.

No matter how often the queen asked the princess what the matter was, she would never tell her; until one day an

urchin crept into the palace and whispered to the queen, 'The princess does not want to go out because she hates to see how poor the people are.'

Now the old queen was very, very rich. So she gave more than half her wealth away. She still had plenty for herself and there was enough to make her subjects happy.

With the people smiling happily, the princess enjoyed going out among them and when the queen resigned, Helena became a popular ruler.

February **29**

THE WILD GOOSE

Every winter a flock of wild geese flew over Anna's house, flying off to warmer places.

Anna always looked out for them and one day when she was playing in her garden, she heard the sound of their calls in the sky. She looked up and saw the flock overhead.

Suddenly one of the beautiful birds fell to the ground, right in front of Anna's feet. She saw immediately that its wing was broken.

All winter she cared for it and when spring was coming she heard the flock of wild geese flying back from their warm holiday, back home to where they usually lived. Anna ran into the house and carried the goose into the garden. As soon as it saw the rest of the geese, it flapped its wings and flew up to join its brothers and sisters. Anna was quite sad to see her goose go, but she knew it would be happier with the other birds.

March **1**

THE BRAVE QUEEN

'I am the bravest person in the world,' the queen boasted to her noblemen after a great battle. 'None of you are as brave as me.'

The next year the queen was at war again, this time not against soldiers but a plague of wasps. Brave Queen Theresa was unafraid of them and left her palace, her face covered with fine gauze. In her hand she held smoking torches which forced the wasps away.

'I am the bravest person in the land,' the queen boasted to her nobles afterwards. 'None of you would face the wasps. I was not afraid.'

Next day the courtiers were astonished to hear cries of help coming from the queen's chamber.

They ran in and there was the queen atop a stool, with mice all around.

'Get them away from me!' she cried.

The courtiers quickly obliged and funnily enough the queen never boasted about how brave she was ever again.

March 2

MOTHER PUSSYCAT

One day, a farmer's wife noticed that her goose had laid twelve eggs in her nest. She went and picked up her bird and told it to sit on the nest until the eggs had hatched.

After a while, the goose got tired of sitting on her eggs and called on the farm cat, 'I'm terribly sore sitting on these eggs for so long. I simply must stretch my legs. Please keep the eggs warm for me while I go for a walk.'

The cat settled herself on top of the eggs and kept them warm with her fur.

On her walk, the goose met some friends and was having such a good gossip that she forgot all about the eggs. In the meantime the cat's fur was so warm that the eggs hatched.

The little goslings were very surprised to find that their mother was a cat. From that day on they followed the cat all over the farmyard, wherever she went, much to the surprise of the farmer's wife.

March 3

WOODKIN

One day a farmer picked up his knife and carved a little baby from a beech branch. He took it into the kitchen and gave it to his wife, who began to cry at the sight of the little wooden baby. One of her tears fell on the carving and it came to life.

The woman rushed and found some milk to give to the child. The baby

drank it all up and asked for more. And more . . . and more . . . and more . . . All the while the baby grew and grew.

There was soon nothing left to feed Woodkin (that was the name that the couple had decided to call their child), so he waddled outside into the farmyard.

Unfortunately he slipped and fell over. He had become so large that he could not right himself and the old man and lady were forced to leave him there.

The next morning when the couple went into the yard they were astonished to find a fine beech tree growing where Woodkin had fallen. They cared for it lovingly and every year they cut its fine branches and sold them for firewood. They soon became rich.

March 4

THE MAGIC BOX

Simon and Fiona were all alone in the world. Their father had been killed in an accident and their mother had died shortly afterwards from grief. The only thing that she left them was a box. When they opened it they found a note inside telling them that it was a magic box and if they used the magic words the box would give them all the food they would need.

But before they could read the magic words a gust of wind tore the paper from their hands and blew it into the fire.

Just then there was a knock on the door and an old lady came into the house. 'I am starving,' she said. 'Give me a little something to eat.'

'Of course,' said Fiona and ran to the kitchen. She picked up the last piece of bread and gave it to the old lady, who took it gratefully and asked the children why they were not eating with her.

'Why? Because we have nothing left,' said Simon.

'Such kindness must be repaid,' said the old lady.

Suddenly she was transformed into the most beautiful lady the children had ever seen. She was their fairy godmother and was so happy at how good they were she told them the magic words.

As soon as she spoke to them she disappeared and the children never saw her again but they remembered her for ever.

March 5

SOLDIER, SOLDIER

There was once a girl who fell in love with a soldier, but when she asked him

to marry her he said he could not, for he had no coat to put on. So the girl gave him one.

Again she asked him to marry her, but he said he couldn't, for he had no socks. So the girl gave him some.

Again she asked him to marry her, but he said he couldn't because he had no hat, no gloves and no breeches. And each time the girl gave him what he was lacking.

Eventually the soldier was in fine clothes.

'Oh soldier, soldier, will you marry me, with your musket, fyfe and drum?' To which the soldier replied: 'Oh no, pretty maid, I cannot marry you, for I have a wife at home.' And off he marched.

THE STORY OF THE LONELY KID

There was once a lonely kid who could not make friends with any of the other animals. He became lonelier and lonelier until one day he decided to leave the farm.

For days and days he walked until he came to the outskirts of a great city. He was very afraid, for he had never been in a city before, but taking all his courage in both horns he entered the city. He had never heard such noise before. No matter where he went there was hustle and bustle and noise. It was too much to bear, so the little kid took to his heels and ran back home.

'Where have you been?' all the animals asked. 'We missed you so much.'

'I never knew you would miss me. You never talked to me when I was here before.'

'That's only because we were shy. But now that you're back we promise to try and be friends. Don't go away again.'

So the kid promised to stay on the farm and lived happily forever after.

March 7

THREE LITTLE FARMYARD BIRDS

There was once a farmer's wife who was very short sighted. One day her hen and her goose and her duck all hatched eggs at the same time. The chicken, the gosling and the duckling were so alike that the farmer's wife could hardly tell them apart.

'Why don't you knit them different coloured caps?' joked the farmer.

Now the farmer had only said that as a joke. He really thought that it was time his wife bought some spectacles. But the woman took him seriously.

The three little birds were very proud of their hats and went for a walk in them. But everyone who saw them said, 'How silly. Whoever heard of birds wearing hats.'

Now the farmer's wife did not like everyone laughing at the birds, because she really knew that they were laughing at her. So putting her vanity to one side she went and bought some glasses. And even she laughed when she saw the silly hats on the birds.

March 8

STELLA THE STAR

Stars live to be very old — very old indeed. When Stella the star was three million years old, which is very young for a star, she had to go to school to learn to count. But try as she would she could not sit still in the classroom.

'Stella,' her teacher would say. 'Do sit still.'

Eventually the teacher became very angry with her, picked her up and threw her out of the classroom into the dark blue sky outside.

It was a lovely sensation, floating through the air; and millions of miles below men and women on Earth looked up and saw Stella shooting through the night sky.

'Why,' they said to each other. 'There's a shooting star.'

So if you ever see a star flying through the sky, it's probably Stella, who is having a much better time than she had in class trying to sit still during her Arithmetic lesson.

March 9

THE THREE FAIRIES AND THE FARMER'S TWELFTH SON

A farmer once had eleven sons. When a twelfth boy was born he couldn't help wishing that it had been a girl. And he said to his wife, 'What are we going to call him? We've run out of names!'

Just then three fairies appeared by the cradle.

'I grant him wisdom,' said the first.

'I grant him a stout heart,' said the second.

'And I grant him . . .' the third began, but the farmer stopped her.

'The first thing this boy needs is a name,' he said.

'He can be called anything,' said the third fairy. 'Giving names is not part of our job.'

Then, before the farmer could interrupt again, she said,

'I grant him that he shall be earnest.'

'That's more like it,' said the farmer, and immediately he christened his twelfth son Earnest!

March 10

THE ELEPHANT AND THE HERRING GULL

There was once a herring gull who made friends with an elephant. The two would play together every day, until the time came for the bird to fly off home.

'I wish I could fly,' said the elephant one day.

The bird began to flap its wings and slowly it left the ground. It flew around the elephant and said, 'Now you try by flapping your ears.'

All of a sudden there was a mighty 'WOOOOSH' and the elephant was hovering above the ground.

'Now move your ears this way,' said the gull.

The elephant did so and moved higher off the ground.

He looked down and everything looked very small.

'How do I land?' he cried.

The bird showed him and a few seconds later the elephant was on the ground.

'I don't think elephants were made to fly,' he said. 'Still it's nice to know I can do it if I really want to.'

And the gull said, 'Most things can be done if you really want them and try hard enough.'

March 11

LILY THE LAMB

There was once a lamb called Lily who kept leaving the rest of the flock and wandering off.

One day the farmer's wife had a wonderful idea and hung a bell round the lamb's neck.

'What's this for?' Lily asked Shep the dog.

'I don't know,' said Shep.

The next day, Lily wandered off from the rest of the herd, as usual. But this time the farmer found her almost as soon as she had gone.

The next day the same thing happened, and the next and soon Lily found

that it was no fun playing hide-and-seek with the farmer, for he always found her as soon as she had gone. She never found out why. But we know, don't we?

March 12

THE PRINCESS'S TEARS

Poor Princess Pearl. She simply could not stop crying. If ever anyone was unkind to her she would burst into tears of sadness, and if anyone was nice to her she would burst into tears of happiness.

Everyone soon became very fed up with Princess Pearl and her tears. This made the Princess cry even more.

Now apart from crying, the only other

thing she did well was to play the trumpet. One day she was so moved by the tune she was soon in tears.

Suddenly a little dwarf appeared before her.

'Who are you?' asked the princess.

'The dwarf who can't cry,' said the little fellow. 'I've come to ask you if I can have some of your tears.'

'Of course,' said the princess.

The little dwarf said a few magic words and the princess immediately stopped crying. And after that she only cried half as much as she had before and everyone was much happier.

March 13

THE RAINBOW DWARF

It had been raining very hard, but then the sun had come out and a beautiful rainbow had appeared.

Jimmy was happily splashing through the puddles when he saw the lovely rainbow.

He began to count the colours.

Red, Orange, Yellow, Green, Blue, Indigo and Violet. 'That makes seven, in all,' he said to himself. 'I wish I could remember them.'

All of a sudden a little rainbow dwarf appeared on his shoulders and said, 'I know a way.'

'What's that?' Jimmy asked.

'Just say to yourself Richard Of York Gained Battles In Vain. And the first letter of each word is the same as the first letter of the colours. Try it.'

And it works, you know.

March 14

COCO AND MAMIE

'Why don't you go up into the attic and dress up in old clothes?' suggested Peter and Kathy's mother, one rainy day.

Tea was nearly ready when strange sounds came from the stairs. All at once two funny figures came into the kitchen.

'I'm Coco the Clown,' said one, raising his hat with one hand and holding up long, baggy trousers with the other. He had thick red lips which mummy recognized as the same colour as her old lipstick—and a red nose.

'And I am Madame Mamie,' said the other, curtseying in her high-heeled shoes, which were too big for her, and clutching a huge bag.

All through tea Coco and Mamie acted out their roles.

'Do leave some food for Peter and Kathy,' said Peter's mother, but Coco and Mamie ate everything in sight.

I hope Peter and Kathy had something to eat—don't you?

March 15

THE SADDLEMAKER'S MARK

There was once an old saddlemaker who lived in a far-off land with his wife. He worked hard but was very poor until one day war broke out and the demand for saddles increased so much that the saddlemaker had to work from morning till night to meet it.

He wanted to put a mark on every saddle he made so that everyone would know that he had made them. His name was unsuitable because it was too long and difficult to say properly.

One night he went to bed and had a strange dream. He saw a hedgehog sitting astride a fine colourful cockerel. When he wakened up he remembered his dream and suddenly thought what a fine sign that would make for his sad-

dle. The hedgehog was, after all, heavily armoured just like the knight that went off to war. And the cockerel was king of the farmyard, as proud as the fine steeds that carried the knights. And ever since then his saddles carried the sign of the cock and the hedgehog.

The kidnapper ran away as fast as he could and never came back again.

March 17

GRANDDAD'S PRESENT

The day after tomorrow was going to be Billy's birthday. He had already wished for a present: he had wished and wished for nothing else but a knife like Granddad's. But the next day, when he had told his parents, they said that he was too young to have a knife like that. That afternoon, while they were out for a walk, Billy told his grandfather all about it.

'What do you need a knife like that for, Billy?' his grandfather asked.

'So that I can cut off a willow twig to make a whistle like the other boys.'

Granddad smiled, took out his pocket-knife, and cut Billy a willow twig and carved a whistle. Then he shut the knife and gave it to Billy.

Soon Billy could play all sorts of tunes on his whistle. It was the best present he had ever had.

March 16

THE HEDGEHOG'S LUCKY ESCAPE

There was once a rich hedgehog who lived in a wood. He was very popular and had lots of friends.

One day a wicked kidnapper came into the wood determined that he would carry the hedgehog away and hold him to ransom.

He made his way to the hedgehog's home and called, 'Hedgehog, come here, I have a present for you.'

The hedgehog came out of his house and the kidnapper immediately tried to grab him.

But the hedgehog was too quick for him. Quick as a flash he rolled himself up into a ball and rolled himself towards the kidnapper, his sharp prickles pricking his ankles.

March 18

THE MAGIC CRAYONS

Joanna had been given some bright colourful crayons for her birthday.

'What can I draw?' she thought to herself. 'I know, I'll draw a balloon.'

She got to work and had quickly finished her balloon. She decided to put a man in it and gave him a telescope, so that he could see the earth below.

Can you guess what happened next? The picture tells you. The balloon floated off the paper and right out of the window, and Joanna never saw it again.

When she wakened up she thought she had been dreaming, but when she found her drawing pad the balloon had completely disappeared. She had been dreaming—hadn't she?

March 19

THE RAINBOW

'There's a pot of gold at the end of the rainbow,' said Tommy to his friend one day, after it had been raining.

'Let's go and look for it,' said his friend.

The two set out and began to walk towards the end of the rainbow. They walked such a long way, but the rainbow always stayed the same distance away from them.

And then when the sun went in the rainbow faded away and with it the pot of gold. 'We'll never find it now,' said Tommy. 'But never mind, we've had a nice walk, anyway.'

March 20

THE MAN IN THE BALLOON

Remember Joanna's odd dream where her balloon painting drifted out of the window?

Well, as it floated upwards and upwards the man in the balloon looked down with his telescope and saw a lovely empty house. It had ivy growing round the door and a pretty garden with bright spring flowers in the flower bed.

It looked so pleasant that Joanna's

in the garden, she saw that the daffodils and tulips that her father had planted some months before were beginning to flower. She darted back inside and filled up her watering can so that she could give the pretty flowers a drink. 'Spring has really arrived,' she thought happily as she watered the flowers.

March 22

IT REALLY IS SPRINGTIME

Cecily was right, Spring had really arrived. The next day there were even more flowers peeking through the earth than usual and the sun shone warmly.

'Mummy,' she cried. 'Can we have tea in the garden this afternoon? We could wear our coats just in case we catch a chill.'

So that afternoon Mummy and Cecily had tea in the garden at a table that Cecily set under the oak tree.

'Just think, Mummy,' said Cecily, 'we'll soon be able to do this every afternoon without our coats on.'

balloonist decided to float down and live in it.

And as far as Joanna knows, he's still there—and she dreams about him very often.

March 21

THE SWALLOWS OF SPRING

Cecily wakened up as usual one morning and was astonished to hear the sound of swallows singing on the telegraph wires outside her house. She ran across her room, and sure enough, there were her old friends the swallows lined up on the wires.

'You must be awfully tired after your long journey from the warm lands. I'll give you some food. Wait a minute.'

She dressed quickly and ran downstairs into the kitchen, where she collected some nuts and some breadcrumbs and ran outside.

She scattered some bits of breadcrumb and nuts all over the garden and the swallows ate them all up.

When Cecily looked at the swallows

'But we'll have to work hard in the garden to make everything neat and tidy. Will you help us this year?' said Mummy.

'Of course I will,' cried Cecily. And do you know, she did.

March 23

WHY THE DEVIL WALKS WITH A LIMP

In some parts of the world, on Shrove Tuesday, boys and girls dress up as devils and play tricks on each other. One year in a little village in Germany, a real devil slipped into the fun and games.

He asked a boy called Jack to climb on his back and go for a ride.

Jill, Jack's sister, noticed his hoof and shouted a warning to Jack, but Jack didn't hear her and the devil ran off.

Through the village the devil ran with Jack on his back, and Jack began to become quite scared.

'Stop,' he cried.

But the devil rode on.

Jack was really terrified by now. He looked up and saw that they were running through some trees. He managed to pull a branch from one of them and dropped it on the devil's foot. The devil stopped in agony, for the branch had been very heavy. Jack picked it up and banged it hard on the devil's foot, and then ran back to the village. The devil was in such pain that he could not follow him, and has walked with a limp ever since.

March 24

THAT DEVIL AGAIN

The devil did not forgive Jack for hurting his foot and planned his revenge. The next day he went back to the village, wearing shoes to cover his hoof.

'Come, Jill,' he cried. 'Come and have a piggy-back.'

She jumped on his back and away he ran, along the same path.

They were running through the same trees when Jill began to be scared. She tried to stop the devil, but he ran on.

It was just as well that Jill managed to grab some nettles. She knew just where to hold them without being stung. She rubbed them into the devil's face and he dropped her, screaming in agony.

She ran back to the village and the devil ran off to find a doch leave to ease the pain. He never went back to the village again.

March 25

THE PRETTY FLOWER

There was once a flower who thought it was the prettiest flower in the entire world. It had pretty yellow petals and a lovely, deep perfume. It lived beside a lovely pool and it could see its reflection in the water.

'I am,' it thought to itself, 'the most beautiful thing in the world.'

One day a little girl came along and saw the flower. It was so beautiful she couldn't resist picking it and taking it home.

She gave it to her grandmother, who smiled happily when she saw it. Grandmother put it in a lovely vase on top of her dressing table where she could see it. The flower was just as happy because it was near a large mirror and could see itself quite easily.

I wonder if you can guess what its name was? It was Narcissus.

THE SMOKING LION

The circus was very proud of its lion. He could do all sorts of tricks and was the most popular animal in the circus.

One day, unknown to anyone, the lion found a pipe and tobacco and, having seen people smoke, he lit it.

In a few moments the air was black with smoke and all of a sudden one of the trainers came rushing past carrying a ladder, followed by another carrying a bucket of water.

'Where are you rushing off to?' asked the lion.

'There's a fire near here,' shouted the trainer.

'No, there's not. It's me, smoking!'

'Lions shouldn't smoke,' said the trainer.

'But humans do,' retorted the lion.

'Only silly ones. And you're not silly, are you?'

The lion thought about it and then put out his pipe. And do you know— he's never smoked since!

THE GOOSEGIRL

Once upon a time there was a princess called Ella. Unfortunately her mother died and when her father married again, her stepmother was so jealous of Ella's beauty that she sent her away.

Ella travelled far and wide and eventually she got a job tending a farmer's geese. She was very contented and after a few months she fell in love with the farmer's handsome son. The two were married and were so happy that when news came that her stepmother had died, Ella refused to go home.

'I'd much rather be a happy goosegirl than bother about affairs of state,' she said.

51

March 28

THE SCAREHERON

A perch was swimming along one day when suddenly it stopped and blinked in amazement; for there, in the middle of the river, stood a heron, wearing the most ridiculous hat and socks.

'What are you doing there?' it asked the bird. But there was no reply.

'I said, what are you doing there?' it repeated, loudly this time.

Just then the owner of the river walked by with his son. 'Do you like my scareheron?' the boy asked.

'Your what?' said the father.

'My scareheron. I noticed that the birds were flying down and catching your fish. So I made a scareheron—just like the scarecrow in the field.'

'So that's what it is!' thought the fish.

'So that's what I am!' thought the scareheron, ''cos I was wondering too!'

March 29

HOW THE FISHERMAN CAUGHT A MAGPIE

A magpie was flying over a river one day when it spotted something red bobbing in the water. It swooped down and took the object in its mouth, thinking it to be a tasty fish.

But it wasn't!

It was a fisherman's float and the poor magpie found itself caught on the fisherman's line.

The fisherman had been snoring on the bank and woke up when he heard his line being pulled. He was horrified when he saw the poor bird at the end of his line and gently pulled it in.

The magpie allowed itself to be handled by the angler who delicately removed the hook from its throat.

As soon as it was free, the bird flew off and from that day on was very careful never to pick up a float again.

March 30

BREAKFAST SURPRISE

'Do you know what day it is today?' Lucy asked her husband, Jimmy, one morning.

There was no reply.

She left the room and came back a few minutes later carrying a brightly wrapped package. She put it on the table in front of Jimmy.

'What's that?' he asked.

'It was to be a birthday present for someone I know but I don't think I'll give it to him now.'

'Why not?' Jimmy said.

'Because he doesn't even know it's his birthday.'

'Don't be silly,' said Jimmy. 'Everyone knows when their birthday is.'

'When is your birthday, Jimmy?'

Jimmy thought for a second and then said, 'March 30. It's my birthday.'

'Happy birthday,' said Lucy. 'Here's your present.'

'Thank you, I'd quite forgotten,' he said.

'I know,' replied Lucy.

March 31

PRINCE LONESOME

The only place where Prince Oscar ever seemed to be happy was beside an old willow tree, quite close to his palace. In spring when the tree was fully in bud, Prince Oscar would often sit under it and sigh wistfully to himself, 'If only I could find a girl as beautiful as this tree, then I'd be happy.'

One spring he cut off a twig and made himself a whistle. He began to whistle a sad little tune and all of a sudden the tree creaked and a door appeared in its mighty trunk.

The prince couldn't resist opening it and going in. He was astonished to find a beautiful maiden sitting there, spinning.

'Who are you?' he asked in wonder.

'The Princess Willow. A witch cast a spell on me years ago. The sound of

53

your sad whistle has broken the spell and I am free to leave the tree.'

The prince led her out of the tree and into the bright daylight. She was so lovely that he immediately asked her to marry him. She agreed and they lived happily ever after.

April 1

APRIL FOOL

'Mummy,' cried Billy on the first of April, 'come quickly, the stove is on fire.'

Billy's mother ran into the kitchen but there was no sign of any fire.

Some time later Billy's mother called out, 'Billy, come quickly. Granny's just arrived with some lovely ice cream.'

But Billy stayed where he was. He wasn't going to be caught out with such a silly April Fool.

'Quick, Billy, it's melting,' shouted Billy's grandmother.

But Billy stayed out. A few minutes later he went downstairs and there was Mummy and Granny eating the last drop of ice cream.

'Oh Billy, we thought you didn't want any,' said his mother.

Poor Billy. He felt that he was the April Fool.

April 2

GRANDFATHER EEL'S TOOTHACHE

'Oh dear, I've got the most dreadful toothache,' moaned Grandfather Eel. He swam up the river to see the crayfish dentist and when he arrived there the crayfish examined his teeth very carefully.

'I have never seen such dirty teeth,' he said. 'And the tooth that is giving you trouble is so bad I will have to pull it out.'

He told the eel to open his mouth wide, and after giving him something to

you can, and then before you go to bed. And you must brush them carefully.'

And Grandfather Eel was so keen not to lose any more teeth that he brushed his teeth carefully three times a day every day.

MARJORY THE SHEPHERDESS

lessen the pain, he took his pincers and pulled the tooth out.

'When did you last clean your teeth?' the crayfish asked the eel.

'Oh, I can't remember. Last week I suppose,' said the eel.

'Well, if you don't want to lose any more teeth, you must brush them every morning after breakfast, after lunch if

Marjory was a shepherdess and one day she lost one of her sheep. She went to search for it and walked into the forest. She came to a cliff and stopped in amazement, for all around there were shiny marbles.

She picked one up and immediately a raven and a squirrel appeared as if from nowhere.

'Who calls us?' asked the raven.

'I'm sorry,' said Marjory. 'I lost my lamb and I came looking for it.'

'Lost your lamb. Very careless,' squawked the raven. 'Never mind, we'll find it!' And they did just that.

A few minutes later Marjory suddenly woke up, having dropped off in the warm spring sunshine. You don't think she was dreaming, do you?

April 4

HOW FLOWERS GOT ROOTS

Every night the flowers are rocked to sleep by the breeze and Mother Thyme tells them a story. One night she told them how flowers came to have roots.

A long, long time ago, flowers used to move quite freely across the land. But one day it was so hot and dry that a little pansy decided that it could not move another step. It stopped in the shade of a wise old yew tree who told it that if it dug its feet into the ground, it would get some water to drink.

The pansy did just that and was soon quite refreshed. In fact it was so re-freshed that it decided to stay there.

Other flowers passed by and the pansy told them how to get water out of the ground. Soon every flower decided to put down roots to get something to drink.

And that's how flowers got roots.

April 5

THE BAREFOOTED TRAVELLER

'Why are you not wearing any shoes?'

a man asked a barefooted traveller one day.

'I can't afford a pair. But why does this town have no name?'

'We can't agree on one,' replied the man. 'In fact if you can think of one, I'll buy you a pair of shoes.'

The barefooted traveller thought for a second and then said, 'Why not call it Underhill, after all it nestles in the valley beneath these hills.'

'What a splendid name, well done,' said the first man.

'Can I have my shoes now, please?' asked the barefooted traveller.

'No. Why should I give you the shoes?'

'Because we had a bargain,' said the traveller.

'Well, you've learned a lesson, haven't you?' said the man. 'Always make sure that you can trust people you make bargains with,' and he walked off.

April 6

MAGGY AND THE VIOLETS

It was Maggy's mother's birthday and Maggy had decided to pick her a bunch of violets as a special present. She went into the garden and bent down to pluck the first one, when suddenly it said, 'Don't pick me. Smell me instead.'

So Maggy smelt the first violet and it smelt so sweet that she decided to leave it there. But when she bent down to pick the second one, it, too, asked to be smelt and not picked.

What was Maggy to do? What could she give her mother for her birthday?

Suddenly she had a wonderful idea. She went into the kitchen and set a tray with tea things. Then she very carefully made a pot of tea and cut some cake.

When it was ready she called her mother and they both had a special birthday tea in the garden just. beside the violets where they could both enjoy looking and smelling the beautiful spring flowers.

April 7

HOW LILY GOT HER SPOTS

When the little ladybird was born, there was much rejoicing in Rose-Hip Cottage where her parents lived. They decided that the little ladybird should be called Lily.

Her mother sewed her a lovely red apron, just like Little Red Riding Hood's, and told her that if she was a good girl, she would sew black buttons on it — seven in all, like the other ladybirds in her family.

On Monday, Lily was so well behaved that her mother sewed the first button on as a reward. On Tuesday Lily helped with the washing up and she got another button for that. On Wednesday she got another button because she made breakfast, and on Thursday she flew so well the first time she was taken for a flying lesson that she was given her fourth button.

She still had three more to get.

I wonder how she got them.

April **8**

LILY HAS AN ACCIDENT

On Friday Lily had a dreadful accident. She fell over and tore her lovely apron.

'Never mind,' her father said. 'Mummy will sew it for you and you won't even be able to see where the rip was.'

And Lily was so brave when her apron was being repaired that she was given her fifth black button as a special award. She was proud. None of the other ladybirds of her age had half as many buttons as she had.

On Saturday Lily and her father flew into the fields. They floated about in the meadows from flower to flower and said 'Hello' to all the insects that they met on their travels. All the other insects who had never met Lily before were very impressed with her and told her father so. And as soon as they got home, Lily got her sixth button because her father was so proud of her.

Six out of seven. Still one more to go.

April **9**

LILY'S SEVENTH BUTTON

The next day, Lily was taken to the old stump in the middle of the forest glade. There sat the King of the Ladybirds. Lily curtseyed prettily to him.

He asked her her name and then he asked her if she could fly.

'Yes, Sir,' said Lily and flew in a perfectly straight line across the glade.

Then the king said in a very stern voice, 'Lily. You already have been given six of your buttons, but only I can

give you the seventh to show that you are a fully-fledged ladybird.'

Lily's heart almost stopped beating, for she was very nervous.

'Because you have been so good, and can fly so straight, I hereby invest you with your seventh button.'

And all the other ladybirds who were present applauded and Lily blushed as red as her red cloak. She was a fully-fledged ladybird at last, with seven spots like the other ladybirds have.

April 10

THE BLACK FOREST

Once upon a time a fairy lived in a large forest in Germany. She was very shy, so shy, in fact, that she did not even want the sun to see her and she would only come out at night.

But one morning the sun rose just a little earlier than usual and caught sight of the shy fairy. The fairy immediately turned herself into a boar and hid among the great trees.

It happened that on that particular day the Lord of the Forest went hunting and chased a deer past the tree where the fairy, in her boar disguise, was hiding. A long way behind a little fawn ran into the forest to find its mother.

The fairy was so angry that she summoned up every last drop of her magic power and cried, 'Forest, turn black, as black as the night.' The forest immediately became so dark that the hunt had to be abandoned.

Today, it is still called The Black Forest.

April 11

THE PARCHMENT

Once upon a time a young man set off to

make his way in the world. His grandmother gave him a parchment and told him never to unroll it unless he tried every way round a problem.

Unfortunately it was a time of great trouble and turmoil and the lad could find no employment. He became poorer and poorer and ended up living as a down-and-out in the streets of the main town.

He became so miserable that one day he decided to kill himself. He climbed on to a high bridge and was just about to jump off into the water below, when he remembered the parchment that his grandmother had given him.

As a last resort he unrolled it and read the words. They said: 'Never let pride stand in your way. Remember you can always come home no matter what you have done; we will always love you here.'

The words made the young man think again and he climbed down from the bridge and went back home where he was welcomed with open arms by all his family.

THE GOLDEN FISH

One day a fisherman caught a golden fish in the lake.

'Fisherman,' said the fish, 'if you release me I shall grant your every wish.'

The fisherman let the fish go, and when he went home that evening he told his wife, who was doing the washing in the old washtub, what had happened.

'How stupid you are,' she scolded him. 'Go back to the lake at once and tell the golden fish I want a new house.'

The wish was granted. But then the fisherman's wife wanted a fine mansion, and then a royal palace. In the end the proud woman sent her husband to tell

the fish she wanted his castle at the bottom of the lake. The waters parted, and the fish jumped out, slapped his tail against the surface, and disappeared again without a word.

When the fisherman returned home, he found only his old cottage, and in it his wife, doing the washing in the old washtub.

April **13**

PUSSY CAT

Pussy Cat, Pussy Cat,
    where have you been?
I've been up to London
    to look at the Queen.
Pussy Cat, Pussy Cat,
    what did you there?
Well, the queen was out
    so I went to the mayor.
Pussy Cat, Pussy Cat, what did he say?
He said, very nicely,
    'Puss Puss, Good Day.'
Pussy Cat, Pussy Cat,
    did you see his house?
Of course I did — and in it a mouse.
Pussy Cat, Pussy Cat,
    what then did he say?
He said, 'Try and catch it
    and have it for tea.'
Pussy Cat, Pussy Cat, what did you say?
I said, not today — I'm on holiday.
Pussy Cat, Pussy Cat, did he say more?
No, not a word —
    he showed me the door.
Pussy Cat, Pussy Cat,
    what did you then?
I caught a train and came home again.

April **14**

EDITH AND THE MOLE

Edith loved gardening. From morning till night she would work in the rose bed which was where she met the mole.

He had a silky black waistcoat and Edith decided to call him Blackie.

The mole liked nothing better than digging, only it didn't matter to him where he dug. One day two large mounds appeared in the rose beds.

Edith was very upset and the next time she saw the mole she said to him, 'Daddy's very angry with you, you must not dig in the rose bed.'

The mole never dug up the roses again — but there were two mounds in the lawn the next day.

April 15

THE MOLE GETS A JOB

Some distance from Edith's house, there lived a little boy called Anthony who could not walk very well. He spent most of his time sitting at the window, or, if the weather was fine, in the garden.

One day he was in the garden when he saw the ground move! And then a small nose appeared through the soil, and then who do you think poked his head through the soil? Blackie.

He knew that Edith's father would be furious about the lawn, so he had burrowed his way as far as possible from Edith's garden. When he saw the little crippled boy, Blackie immediately felt sorry for him and decided to do some tricks to cheer him up. But after he had done them he realized that he had made a mess, so he picked up a brush and began to clear the mess up.

By the time the boy's father came home from work, the garden was tidier than it ever had been, and he was amazed. He knew his son could not tidy the garden because he was not strong enough. Anthony's father is still puzzled about it. Let's keep Blackie and Anthony's secret, shall we?

April 16

THE LION IN LOVE

There was once a lion that fell in love with the beautiful daughter of a woodcutter. One day he came to ask for her hand in marriage, but, naturally, the woodcutter refused to allow his daughter to marry such a dangerous animal.

The lion then threatened the woodcutter and his wife and the poor couple were terrified. Finally the man said, 'We are greatly honoured by your proposal, but as you can see our daughter is a tender child and if you expressed your affection for her, you may do her injury. Perhaps if you would consent to having your claws removed, it would be safer. Then we may consent to the marriage. And if you had all your sharp teeth pulled out, then we would agree.'

The lion was so in love that he agreed, but when he went back to the woodsman with his claws clipped and his teeth extracted, the man was no longer afraid of him and drove him away.

Love can make people act in a funny way. If you had been the lion, would you have fallen for the woodcutter's trick? I know I wouldn't.

April 17

CHARLIE AND THE GOOSE

Charlie was lying in his hammock one day when he saw a flock of geese fly overhead. 'I wish I could fly like that,' he said to himself.

All of a sudden a lovely white goose landed at his feet and said, 'You cannot fly because you don't have wings, but if you climb onto my back, I will take you for a ride up in the sky.'

Charlie did not wait to be asked again. He climbed on top of the bird's back and soon he was soaring high in the clouds.

Up and up they went and when Charlie looked down, everything looked very small on the ground below. He began to become very frightened. 'Put me down now,' he cried. 'Please take me home.'

But the goose continued to fly up and up and ignored Charlie's pleas. 'I want down,' Charlie cried again.

The goose turned round and said, 'You're mine now, Charlie. We will never land again. We're going to fly in the sky forever.'

April 18

AUNT DOLLY TO THE RESCUE

Charlie was getting more and more frightened. The goose was flying higher and higher and refused to listen to the boy's pleas to let him off.

Suddenly the sky grew dark as a huge shadow passed over the sun. Charlie looked round. There behind him, having grown a pair of powerful wings, was Aunt Dolly, his father's sister, who had been staying with them for a few days.

'Hang on, Charlie,' she shouted, and as she came nearer she picked Charlie off the goose's back and carried him safe-

ly to the ground. But just before they landed, she coughed and dropped him. Charlie landed with a soft plump.

The bump wakened him up, for Charlie had been dreaming. He had been lying on his hammock when the geese flew overhead, and the warm spring sunshine had made him doze off. He had wriggled and turned in his sleep and fallen out of the hammock. He was relieved.

April 19

JOHAN'S PIPE

Johan was a goat-herd. Every morning early, long before the sun came up, he took his father's herd of goats from their house in the valley up to the higher pastures.

All through the day he would whistle loudly and the goats followed him wherever he went and never strayed.

One day, Johan's father gave him a pipe to play his tunes on. But when he tried to make it make music, he couldn't get the notes to sound right, and the goats ran off. So the boy whistled as usual and soon the goats came back.

When he got home that night he told his father what had happened. So Johan was given music lessons and was soon so good at the pipe, that the goats followed him whether he was whistling or playing his pipes.

64

GOOSEY GANDER'S PRESENT

Goosey Gander had lived on the farm for a very long time. She loved the farmer and his wife and all the other animals on the farm. One day, the old sheepdog said, 'It's the farmer and his wife's fiftieth wedding anniversary next week. They're having a big party and everyone will bring them presents.'

'I wish we could give them a present,' said Goosey Gander. 'But that's not really possible, is it?'

The dog nodded in agreement.

Goosey went home sadly and sat on her nest. Her goslings were having an afternoon nap in their beds which Goosey had lined with old feathers.

All of a sudden she had a wonderful idea. She ran to the barn and found a soft sack, and then spent the rest of the day looking for all the feathers she could find. When she told the others what she was doing, they all joined in happily and soon the soft sack was full of the whitest and softest feathers in the farmyard.

Goosey Gander took the sack and left it on the farmhouse doorstep. The old farmer and his wife were so pleased when they saw the gift; it was the softest pillow they had ever slept on and they used it often.

FREDDIE'S FRIENDS

Freddie was a little fox cub who looked just like all his brothers and sisters, but did not behave in the least bit like them. They spent all their time playing pretend fight games when he wanted to play hide and seek. When they were out playing hunt and stalk, he would be looking for someone to play hunt the thimble.

One day when he was on his own as usual, he wandered down to the river bank and met some ducklings there. He let them hold on to his tail with their bright yellow beaks while he swam in the river — and later he let them ride on his back. Then he met some young squirrels and played leap-frog with them for hour after hour.

When it was time to go home for tea, Freddie asked his new friends if he could come back the next day, and what do you think they all said? Why, of course, they all said 'yes' and Freddie was never lonely again.

THE NAUGHTY CROWS

There were once seven crows who were afraid of nothing — especially the scarecrow that Farmer Clone had put in his field. It was made of straw and looked very sad. The crows ignored it completely, and as soon as Farmer Clone scattered some seed and had gone home, they would swoop down and eat it all.

One day Farmer Clone had a bright

idea. He made a new scarecrow and made it look exactly like him. He put a beard on it just like his own, a ragged shirt and trousers like the ones he always wore to work, and a battered hat.

When the crows saw it they laughed and thought, 'Farmer Clone must be silly to think that we'd be scared of that old scarecrow.' But when they swooped down, imagine how surprised they were when the scarecrow came to life and shoo'd them away. For it wasn't a scarecrow at all, it was Farmer Clone himself. And from then on the crows could never be sure if it was the farmer or the scarecrow who was in the field, so they stayed well away from it.

April 23

THE GOLDEN APPLE

There was once a poor peasant girl who went to work in a palace. She was very lovely and as soon as the prince saw her, he fell head over heels in love with her. They were soon married and the prin-

cess sent for her parents so that they could meet their new son-in-law.

When the old couple arrived they were astonished to see what the prince was holding in his hand. 'It's an apple, isn't it?' the man said to his wife.

His wife nodded.

'Well, if he comes to the farm, I'll give him apples by the sackful, and ones more bright gold than that one.'

During the banquet that the prince

had arranged in honour of his wife's parents, the old man asked him to his farm. 'I'll give you sackfuls of apples more bright gold than the one you carry,' said the old man.

The king smiled and handed the old man the golden orb that he was carrying.

The old man took a bite of it, but of course the orb was solid gold and he could not. 'Why, lad,' said the old man. 'Not only will I give you more, at least the apples I will give you are eatable.'

April 24

BRAVE SIR GEORGE

It was a brilliantly sunny day as the knight Sir George rode out to kill the dragon that had been terrorising the kingdom. He couldn't help noticing that his shield caught the bright sunlight and made dazzling patterns on the trees and rocks as he passed.

This gave him an idea. When he reached the dragon's lair he called out, 'Dragon, come out to meet your death.'

The earth trembled as the dragon came out of his cave, breathing fire. As soon as he saw Sir George he ran towards him, flames scorching the grass around the knight. But Sir George shone the sunlight reflected from his shield into the dragon's eyes. The beast was so dazzled that he could not see Sir George as he rode towards him, his lance at full tilt. A few seconds later the dragon lay dead at Sir George's feet and the knight made his way home to a hero's welcome.

April 25

THE PEACOCK'S EYE

Freddy and Billy were playing marbles. The prize was a beautiful peacock's eye marble — the best of all marbles. Freddy was very upset when Billy won it.

As Billy made his way home he passed Freddy's sister, who was wearing a lovely bangle. He suddenly remembered that it was his sister's birthday and he had forgotten to buy her a present.

'I'll swap you something for the bangle,' he said to Jenny.

'I'll give it to you in exchange for that lovely peacock's eye. I know that Freddy wants one,' replied Jenny.

Billy had to agree, for the shops were closed and he could not get a present any other way.

Freddy was so surprised when Jenny came home and gave him the prize marble that he promised to take her turn at doing the washing-up for a whole week.

April 26

THE BEAR IN THE BARREL

There was once a bear that went to steal some honey from the bees. He hid himself in a barrel beside the hive until he saw the swarm fly off, leaving lovely runny honey behind. The bear popped his head out of the barrel and was astonished to see another bear popping its head out of another barrel by the hive.

Both the bears were so guilty at being caught like that that they ran off, which was just as well, for they would have been stung by the guard bees in the hive.

April 27

JOANNA'S NEW TOY

Joanna had a doll called Penny. Every day she played with it from morning to night and Penny loved Joanna as much as Joanna loved Penny. But one day, Penny was left at the end of the bed.

You see, Joanna had had a birthday and had been given a wonderful clown doll. It had bright red lips and a clown's costume.

That night Joanna went to sleep with her clown doll beside her. Poor Penny cried and cried all night. Just before sunrise the clown wakened up and heard Penny crying. He crept quietly down the bed and took Penny's hand. 'Please don't cry. I'll be your friend,' he whispered.

When she woke up, Joanna found her two toys together at the bottom of her bed. 'Oh I'm so glad you're friends,' she

cried. 'Now we can all be friends and play together.'

And from then on they all played together from morning till night.

April 28

BILL AND BOB THE BASSET HOUNDS

Bill and Bob were two basset hounds who were bored one day.

'Why don't we go to play hide and seek with Hoppity the Rabbit?' said Bob. Bill agreed and the two dogs set off.

But when they arrived at Hoppity's house they found all his friends looking very worried. 'We cannot find him any-where,' said Nutkin the Squirrel.

The two dogs, who were very good at organizing things and solving problems, split all the animals into search parties and sent them off in different directions to look for Hoppity. Then they set off by themselves, sniffing for any scent of Hoppity, but there was none at all.

It was getting dark when they had to call off the search and go home.

When they went into their kennel, who do you think was there — curled up and sound asleep? It was Hoppity, who had come to visit them for the day, and had fallen asleep waiting for them.

April 29

TOMMY AT THE FAIR

On the same day every year the fair came to town. As soon as the fair was open for business, Tommy would be there and he always headed straight for the Merry-Go-Round. He always had enough money for five rides. His mother payed for one and his father for another. His aunt and uncle always paid for another two, and he usually managed to pay for one himself.

But this year he had been saving so hard that he had enough money for ten rides. The first five were great fun, but on the sixth Tommy began to feel a bit queezy. On the seventh he turned a little green and on the eighth he felt sick.

He decided not to have his ninth and tenth rides and when the Merry-Go-Round man asked him why, Tommy said, 'Well, you can have too much of a good thing, can't you? It's a lesson I have only just learned.'

April 30

THE WOODCUTTER AND THE THREE AXES

A woodcutter was once chopping down trees by the lakeside. As evening began to fall, he was so tired that he let the axe slip out of his hand, and it fell into the lake.

'How am I to make a living without an axe?' the woodcutter asked himself.

'Here you are,' said a water nymph, rising out of the water. And she threw a solid silver axe at the woodcutter's feet.

'It's not mine,' said the woodcutter.

'Is this yours, then?' asked the nymph and she threw a gold axe onto the bank.

'No, that's not mine, either,' sighed the woodcutter.

Finally the nymph threw out the woodcutter's own axe.

'That one's mine!' cried the delighted woodcutter.

'You are such an honest man,' the water nymph told the woodcutter, 'so you shall have all three as a reward.'

May 1

THE KIND SUN

One evening the sun was just about to go to bed and close the shutters of the tower he lived in, when he noticed three little birds crying closeby.

'Why are you crying?' he asked them.

'We were out flying on our own for the first time and we can't find our way home. We know that we're not far, but you are going to bed now and we won't be able to find our way home in the dark,' they all chirped together.

Now the sun had had a very long day and was quite tired. Also he knew that a lot of people depended on him going to bed at a definite time each night. However he thought that they wouldn't

mind, just this once, if he was a few minutes late in going to bed. So he shone just long enough for the three birds to find their way home.

And a lot of people did wonder why the sun was so late going to sleep, but I'm sure they would not have minded at all if they knew the reason why. Don't you?

May 2

THE TWO BROTHERS

A wicked magician once captured two brothers. If ever they tried to leave his ship, they would be transformed into seagulls — only becoming human again when they returned to the ship.

One day one of the brothers had an idea. He explained it to his brother and then swam ashore where he was turned into a seagull. His brother watched him fly overhead and then called the magician. He kept him talking long enough for the seagull to fly into the magician's cabin and find the spell in his book. He ripped it out with his beak and flew off.

When he saw that the magician had gone back to his cabin, the seagull swooped down and dropped the spell at his brother's feet. The magic words were immediately said and the spell was broken.

The two lads swam ashore and never saw the wicked magician again.

May 3

JACK AND THE GOAT

A boy called Jack set out with his goat one day to make his fortune. An old man joined him and asked if he could share his humble meal.

'Of course,' said Jack.

'You are a good lad, Jack,' said the old man. 'I must reward you,' and he said some magic words. Immediately Jack's goat became bright blue, his beard became red and his horns became red, with white and blue stripes.

'That's a reward?' said Jack. 'I'd hate to see a punishment.'

'Take the goat to the castle on the other side of this forest,' said the wizard. 'There you will get your reward.'

With nothing to lose, Jack led his funny-looking goat through the forest. He came to a castle and on its gate he saw this notice: 'WHOSOEVER CAN MAKE THE PRINCESS LAUGH WILL MARRY HER.'

Jack climbed onto the goat's back and rode across the drawbridge. The princess saw him and immediately laughed for the first time in her life.

In fact, it was the odd-looking goat she was laughing at, but as princesses cannot marry goats, she married Jack instead and they lived happily ever after.

May 4

THE MAGIC PEA

There was nothing in the world that Rob liked better than peas. One day his mother gave him a bowl of pea pods to shell, for supper. One by one he picked the peas out of the pod and suddenly one of them slipped from his fingers and rolled across the floor. Rob immediately ran off after it.

The pea rolled right out of the kitchen and into the garden. As it rolled it became bigger and bigger and bigger, until it was as large as Rob himself.

Rob ran after it and then froze in his tracks as the pea stopped and began to roll in the opposite direction, chasing Rob as fast as Rob had been chasing him. Rob ran and ran and ran, until he managed to climb a tree to safety and watched as the pea rolled away. As far as he knows it's rolling still.

May 5

REFLECTIONS

Two little birds sat on the banks of a lake one evening just as it was getting dark. They watched, enchanted, as one by one the stars came out. Then one of the birds noticed that the stars were shining in the lake as well as in the sky.

'Look,' it chirped to its friend, and pointed to what it had noticed.

'No,' said the other bird, who was older and wiser. 'They're not shining in the pool, they're reflections of the stars in the sky. If we fly over the lake tomorrow when it's light, we will be able to see our own reflections.'

The next morning that's exactly what they did and they had great fun looking down and seeing their reflections.

Next time you are by a pond, look in and you'll see yourself looking back at you! But don't lean too far or you'll fall into the pond.

May 6

THE FISHING COMPETITION

The river that flowed through the forest was teeming with fish, and lots of the animals who lived there could catch the fish quite easily with their paws.

But there was a little bear cub who couldn't do it properly. He sometimes dipped his paws in too carelessly and the fish were able to swim away, or he over-balanced and fell in, frightening away all the fish and annoying all the other animals fishing nearby.

One day he was strolling through the forest when he came across six fisher-men. They were so scared when they saw the bear cub that they ran off imme-diately, leaving their rods behind.

The cub picked up the first rod and a plump salmon came out of the water. When he picked up the second, the same thing happened—and with the third, fourth, fifth and sixth. There were six lovely salmon and when the bear took them home the animals voted him Fisherman of the Forest!

May 7

THE WHITE HORSE

There was once a knight who had a mag-nificent white horse. He was out riding on it one day when a wicked witch saw it and decided that she wanted the horse for herself.

She knew the knight would never give

it to her if she asked him for it, so she immediately transformed herself into a beautiful maiden and laid down in the bridle path.

A few moments later the knight rode past and saw the maiden. He immediately stopped his horse and dismounted. He carried the maiden to a nearby seat and revived her.

While he was doing this, the maiden cast a silent spell on the horse, causing it to trot quietly away to a spot where only she knew it would be.

As soon as she knew the horse was well out of sight, she changed herself back into a witch. The knight was aghast when he realized he had been tricked.

'Never trust a pretty face,' cackled the witch.

'I never will again,' said the knight as he went sadly home.

THE FLEET-FOOTED FROG

One day a fox went to a lake to drink. A large frog was sitting there and the fox said, 'Be off with you or I shall catch you. You cannot run as fast as I.'

'I'll race you to town, and if I get there before you, promise you'll never come back here again,' said the frog.

The two animals began their race. The frog let the fox get a little way ahead and then, with one enormous leap, jumped lightly on the fox's tail. The fox never felt a thing and ran on towards the town gate. A few yards from the town gate the frog took an almighty leap right over the fox's head and when the fox stopped at the gate—there was the frog waiting for him.

The fox was astonished, but kept his side of the bargain and never went near the pool again.

The frogs still talk about it to this day!

May 9

THE LOST BALL

One day Angela lost her ball in the woods. She put it down while she went to pick flowers and forgot where she had left it.

Two little squirrels found it and thought at first it was something to eat, but when they licked it, it tasted very nasty.

Just then a bird flew overhead. 'It's a ball,' it chirped, 'children play with them. Angela left that one there and she can't remember where she left it.'

So the two squirrels, who felt a bit sorry for Angela, rolled it to where she would easily find it.

Next day Angela was surprised to find her ball so easily.

May 10

THE FUSSY KING

There was once a king who liked good food. One day a new kitchen boy was told to take the king's lunch up to him. There were two covered dishes on the stove—both exactly the same. 'Hurry up,' shouted the chef, so the boy picked up the first one and carried it up to the king.

The king uncovered the dish. The kitchen boy looked horrified as he saw that he must have picked up the wrong dish, for there, on the dish, was half a dozen sausages and a black pudding!

'What's this?' asked the king, who had never even seen a sausage before. 'Smells delicious.' And before the boy could stop him, the king had eaten a whole sausage.

'Delicious,' he said and from then on he had ordinary sausages every day at least once.

May 11

THE GOLDEN FARMSTEAD

There was once a farmer who had two sons. One day he said to them, 'Go out into the world and whichever of you returns with the most beautiful bride will inherit my farm.'

They both set off. 'You need not bother,' said the older to the younger. 'I am bound to win a more beautiful bride.'

They parted shortly after. The young man knew that what his brother had said was true and sat down and wept. A frog hopped by and asked what was the matter. When the lad told the frog, the frog took him to a cavern where there was a beautiful maiden. 'This is my daughter. Take her to your father and if you win the farm, I will be released from the spell that makes me a frog.'

The girl was dressed in shabby rags, but the youth took her home. His brother was there with another beautiful girl dressed in rich silk. The father could not decide which was the more beautiful, so he asked them both to dance. As they did so the rich silks fell from the brother's fiancée, and she was seen to be wearing filthy underclothes. The rags fell from the frog's daughter and she was seen to be wearing spotless, silk undergarments. The father immediately chose the younger son's bride. He inherited the farm and the frog was released from the spell.

May 12

THE FUNFAIR

I looked out of my window
And saw a wonderful sight.
A fair had come to visit us
With tents of red and white.

The merry-go-round had started,
The music sang out loud.
A little man with red balloons
Was standing in the crowd.

The ice cream was delicious,
Strawberry, raspberry, lime;
The roundabout whizzed me round and
round, I had a marvellous time.

May 13

MICKY'S DUVET

Micky was tucked up in bed one night,

his feather-filled duvet keeping him snug and warm. His mother was just saying 'Goodnight', when Micky asked her what the duvet was filled with.

'Feathers,' answered his mother.

That night Micky dreamed that he was playing in the fields when a large eagle swooped down and picked him up in its talons. Micky was whisked up and up and taken to the eagle's nest where there were five chicks. Micky was dropped into the nest beside them and the eagle flew off to find something to eat for her brood. The nest was on the ledge of a cliff and Micky had a wonderful view of the surrounding countryside. All of a sudden the eagle came back with a mouthful of worms and tried to push them into Micky's mouth. Micky woke up shouting and his mother came rushing up to his room. 'What's the matter?' she asked. 'Had a bad dream?'

'Well, it was alright until the bird tried to feed me . . .'

May 14

THE COWHERD

Heidi was a little girl who lived in Switzerland, where she looked after her father's herd of cattle. One day she was very thirsty, but she had forgotten to bring anything to drink with her. The stream was quite far away and it was so hot that Heidi could not be bothered to walk to it. 'Oh dear,' she sighed. 'I'm so thirsty and there's nothing to drink.'

Just then one of the cows came up to her and licked her face. 'I can give you something to drink,' it seemed to say.

Heidi looked at the cow. 'Of course you can,' she said. And she milked some of the cow's milk into her mug. It was delicious.

'How funny,' she thought. 'There was plenty to drink all the time. Isn't it odd that the most obvious things stare us in the face and we never notice them?'

May 15

THE LION WITH A LONG MEMORY

There was once a lion as big and fierce and as strong as all lions. One day, a long sharp thorn went into its paw. The thorn hurt so much that the lion could only limp along and could no longer hunt. When it was in danger of starving to death, it came upon a young man. His name was Androcles. He was a runaway Roman slave and he carried no weapons to defend himself against the hungry lion.

Imagine the young man's amazement when the huge lion held out its paw to him! Androcles saw the terrible thorn and, very gently, he pulled it out, and the lion padded away into the desert.

Much later, Androcles was captured and condemned to be killed and eaten by a lion. But, lo and behold, the lion would not touch him. Can you guess why? Yes, it was the very same lion that Androcles had saved in the desert, and the lion had remembered him!

May 16

SPAGHETTI FOR SUPPER

The Crow family loved worms for supper. One day the lady who owned the garden where the Crows lived put some spaghetti on her kitchen window-sill to cool. Mrs Crow flew past and thought, 'Ah, what lovely worms.' She flew down and took a beakful back to her chicks. They squeaked with pleasure when they

saw the worms but as soon as they tasted them they spat them out in disgust. They tasted of garlic.

Oh well, I don't suppose that the children who lived in the house would have liked worms for their supper, so why should the chicks have liked the spaghetti.

May 17

THE RECITAL

Fiona Frog's cousin was a very famous cellist. She often boasted to her friends that the famous Frederick Frog, cellist, was her cousin, so you can imagine how excited she was when he called one day and said that he would like to visit her.

Fiona Frog asked all her friends round to meet her famous cousin and when the great day arrived they all turned up wearing their best frocks. After tea Fiona Frog asked her cousin if he would play for them all. 'Of course,' he said. 'But first I must tell you what the King of Spain said about my playing when I gave a recital at his palace.' And Frederick Frog told them all how wonderful the King of Spain had thought him . . . and the King of Belgium . . . and the Queen of England . . . and the King of Norway. In fact, he talked for so long about how good everyone said he was that it became too late for anyone to stay to hear him play and they all went home.

Next time he asked to come for tea, Fiona Frog told him not to bother. I wonder why?

May 18

THE FOX'S SUPPER

A fox once stood behind a tree.
Waiting very patiently.
He listened for a quack or cluck.
For that would mean a hen or duck.

The fox that stood so silently
Was waiting for his tea, you see.
Some thoughtless bird may pass
—and then
It's duck for tea, or maybe hen.

I wonder who will have the luck.
The fox, the hen, perhaps the duck.
I hope for both the birds' own sake
The fox gets nothing and has to bake.

May 19

THE DRAGONFLY

Two mosquitoes were getting married and they asked the dragonfly to go and tell all the other insects in the wood of the ceremony and the reception that was to follow it.

The dragonfly flew low over the water and buzzed with all her might so that everyone would hear the news.

Once she had told the bumble-bee she thought that that was everyone, but then she remembered the woodwasps. So she flew off to tell the woodwasps. Then she flew off to tell the mayfly, whom she'd forgotten about. She began to worry that she would miss the reception, but there were so many insects to tell, and she wanted to make sure that everyone was invited.

And the dragonfly has stayed that way. Just watch her on a summer day as she rushes off in one direction and then suddenly stops. That's in case she's just thought it was time to be getting back to the wedding.

May 20

COPPELIA

There was once a boy called Franz who

was in love with a girl called Swanhilda. They lived in a village near the house of Doctor Coppelius.

One day a girl appeared at Doctor Coppelius's window. 'That must be his niece, Coppelia,' everyone said.

Franz passed by and saw her. She was so lovely that he forgot about Swanhilda and began to show off in front of the girl. But no matter what he did, the beautiful Coppelia never moved.

The doctor came out of his house and saw Franz. He went into the inn and said something to the innkeeper. The innkeeper repeated it to the butcher, and soon everyone in the village was in the square watching Franz trying to entertain the girl in the window. They all burst out laughing. 'Why do you all laugh so?' he asked.

'Because it's not a real girl, it's a doll that the doctor built,' said Swanhilda. 'And if you're silly enough to fall in love with a doll, I don't think I want to marry you after all.'

But Franz realized what a fool he'd been and eventually Swanhilda forgave him, and they were married and lived happily ever after.

May 21

THE SHEPHERD BOY AND THE CHEESE

There was once a young shepherd boy who wanted to get married. He knew three sisters, each one prettier than the next, but he didn't know which to choose.

He asked his mother's advice and she told him, 'Invite them all to eat some cheese with you. And when they come, watch carefully how they cut it.'

The young man did as his mother suggested. The first sister ate the cheese, rind and all. The second quickly cut off

the rind, but because she did so quickly and carelessly, she threw away a good part of the cheese with it.

The third sister carefully pared the rind off and not a drop of cheese was wasted. When he told his mother this, she said, 'Marry the third.'

He did so and the happy couple lived joyfully ever after.

May **22**

FIREFLY LANTERN

Late one evening, Little Albert was lying in bed. He was about to go to sleep when he glanced out of the window and saw a shower of sparks in the darkened garden.

'Granny! Come quickly,' he cried.

'Don't worry,' said Granny when she saw what the matter was. 'They're only fireflies.'

She explained that fireflies were little flies that glowed in the darkness because they had little lanterns in their tails.

'I would love a lantern of my own,' said Albert.

'Well, it's your birthday quite soon,' said Granny. 'Maybe someone will buy you one.'

And a few days later when Albert unwrapped a big parcel that said, 'HAPPY BIRTHDAY, ALBERT, LOVE FROM

GRANNY' on it, what do you think was inside it? Yes. A lantern.

May 23

THE KIDS, THE GOAT AND THE WOLF

'Do not open the door to anyone,' said the goat to her kids one day as she was about to go out shopping.

But a wolf had been listening and heard her words. He went to the butcher's shop, stole a goatskin and put it on. He then went back to the cottage and knocked on the door. 'It is your mother, let me in,' he said. But the kids recognized his voice and refused to let him in.

So the wolf went to a merchant and stole a big piece of chalk. He ate it and his voice grew softer. He then stole some flour from the baker and made his face white.

He went back to the cottage again. When the kids heard her soft voice and peeked through the door and saw her white face, they knew it was their mother. But fortunately just as they opened the door, their real mother came round the corner. As soon as she saw the wolf, she put her head down and butted him in the rear before he could get away. It was many months before the wolf showed his face in the woods again.

May 24

THE THREE GOATS

Three goats went into the woods to eat the fresh green leaves there. The first goat had one horn, the second had two and the third had three.

The goat with one horn finished eating first and set off for home. On the way she met a wolf. 'Leave me alone,' cried the goat. My brother with two horns will pass this way soon and his flesh is sweeter.'

The wolf let the first goat go on its way and lay in wait for the second. 'Leave me alone,' cried the second goat when the wolf attacked it. 'My brother with three horns will be along soon. His flesh is much sweeter than mine.'

So the wolf decided to wait for the third goat. But when it came trotting along, the wolf looked at its three sharp horns and hesitated before attacking. The goat took one look at the wolf and charged towards him, butting him high into the air. When the wolf landed, with a loud 'THUMP', how he wished he had not been greedy, and had taken the first goat when he had the chance.

May 25

THE PRINCE AND THE FISH

Prince Rudolf went to the lakeside one day to take a swim. On the banks of the lake he came across a stranded fish. He immediately threw it back in the water and the fish disappeared beneath the waves.

As the prince swam, his ring became loose on his finger and it slipped off and sank to the bottom of the lake. Although the water was deep, it was so clear that Rudolf could see it on the bottom, glimmering in the dappled light. But it was so deep, he could not swim down to it.

Sadly he left the water and dressed. His father and mother would be furious when they found out that he had lost his ring. It had been in the family for centuries and was always worn by the crown prince.

Just as he was about to leave the lakeside, he was astonished to see the fish that he had thrown into the water a few minutes earlier come splashing through the surface with his ring in its mouth.

'After all,' the fish seemed to be saying, 'one good turn deserves another.'

May 26

THE SUN AND THE OLD LADY

Once upon a time there was an old lady who lived in a castle. She was very unhappy because no one ever came to see her. Her only friend was her old cat. 'Oh Puss,' she would often say, 'I wish we could have some visitors.' But the cat only mewed. 'We used to have such happy times when my husband was alive,' she would go on. 'But after he died people stopped coming here.'

One day the old lady called the cat, but it did not come as usual. She decided that she would draw the curtains that had been closed ever since her husband died. All of a sudden sunlight flooded into the room. The old lady looked around and there was the cat, hiding in a corner. The curtains in all the other rooms were closed and the old lady could not help but notice how gloomy her house was. She decided that the time had come to draw back all the cur-

tains and let the sun back into her life.

And soon people came to call on her and her life was once again filled with laughter, as well as sunlight.

May 27

THE SWALLOW'S ADVICE

A farmer was sowing his field one day while a swallow and some other birds sat on the fence watching him.

'Beware of the man,' said the swallow.

'Why?' asked the other birds.

'The farmer is sowing hemp seeds,' said the swallow. 'It is most important that you pick up every seed that he drops. You will live to regret it if you do not.'

But the silly birds payed no attention to the swallow and when spring came the hemp had grown well. And when it was harvested, the hemp was made into cord, and from the cord some nets were made.

And many of the birds that had re-fused to heed the swallow's advice were caught in the nets made of the very hemp that was grown from the seeds they had failed to pick up.

So remember that unless the seeds of evil are destroyed, they may grow to destroy us.

May 28

IDLE JACK

Idle Jack lived with his mother, who was very poor. Idle Jack was not only idle, he was also very vain. He was a good-looking lad and despised the rags that he wore.

'Mother,' he would often ask, 'can I have some money to buy clothes?'

'Don't be silly,' his mother would say. 'We have just enough money to live on, where would I get money to buy you fine clothes?'

One day, Jack's uncle died and left Jack some money. He went into town and bought a green smock and fine green shoes. He spent the rest of the money on a pair of fine red trousers.

'How handsome I look,' he thought to himself as he walked home. 'Mother will be proud of her son when she sees me.'

But when he got home his mother was furious. She slapped him round the ears and sent him straight back to the town to sell his clothes back to the tradespeople.

'Fine feathers don't make fine birds, you know!' she cried after him. And she was right. Fine feathers don't make fine birds.

May 29

THE ORPHAN GIRL AND THE STAG

There was once a little girl who had a wicked stepmother. Every day she was forced to stay in the pastures till evening fell. And when she went home in the evening all that there was to eat was the remains of her stepmother's supper.

One day a stag came up to her, while she was tending her cows. He bent down tamely and opened up one of his antlers. The girl found that inside there was more food than she could possibly eat.

That evening when the girl did not eat her supper, the stepmother asked her why. When she heard the story, she cried, 'Liar,' and sent the girl from the house.

The girl wandered into a clearing in the forest where she found the stag. He bent down and touched her with his antlers and she changed into a beautiful hind. And then the stag and the hind were married and lived happily ever after.

May 30

THE FOX AND THE CAT

One day in a forest a fox and a cat met each other.

'Good day, fox,' said the cat. 'How are you today?'

The fox scowled disdainfully at the cat and spent a good few minutes considering whether or not he ought to reply to such a lowly creature.

'You dare speak to me?' he said

finally. 'I, the mighty fox, the cleverest animal in the world. Renowned for my cleverness, and you, a cat, dare speak to me.'

'At least I can jump into trees to escape danger.'

'And what good is that, please?' asked the fox.

Just then a pack of hounds could be heard barking in the distance. The cat immediately climbed a tree, and the fox took to his heels.

'Now you know the answer,' cried the cat to the fleeing figure of the fox.

May 31

THE RAKE AND THE SCYTHE

A farmer went to market one day and bought a splendid new rake and scythe. When he got home he threw the old rake and scythe into a dark shed. The two implements were furious at this treatment and ran away to find new work.

They walked and walked until they reached the hills where an old shepherd lived. When he saw the rake and the scythe, he was delighted. 'Just what I needed,' he cried and took them into his house, where he cleaned and polished them both and honed the scythe.

The next day he took them out to work. How proud the rake was when it got to work in the grass, raking up the dead leaves and bits of dirt. 'Why, you're the best rake I've ever had,' said the farmer. And he said the same about the scythe, too, as it swished its way through the long grass. 'Just because things are old, doesn't mean that they're useless.'

June 1

THE FALSE PRINCESSES

There was a time when war broke out in King Jollifant's kingdom. A young lad called Peter rallied the king's troops and drove the enemy from the land. As a reward the king told him that he could marry his daughter, Princess Mary, but because Peter came from humble stock the princess was unwilling to marry him.

She persuaded her father to put Peter to the test. 'Have some perfect images of me made,' she said. 'I will sit among them and if he can pick me out as a true princess then I will marry him.'

Peter was led into a chamber where Princess Mary sat among some perfect models of herself.

Peter looked at the models and whis-

pered something to a courtier. A few seconds later the courtier came into the room and released a wasp that Peter had asked him to catch. The wasp flew from model to model, but when it landed on the princess she screamed and shooed it away. Peter knew that she was human as soon as she moved and he claimed her as his bride.

June 2

CLARE'S BIRTHDAY PRESENT

One fine morning, Clare opened her eyes and found a beautiful new doll's pram at the side of her bed. She had never seen the pram before and had heard no one bring it into her room. She took her favourite doll from her shelf and put it into the pram.

Then she wheeled the pram across the landing and into Mummy and Daddy's room. They were sitting up in bed when she went in, having a cup of tea.

'Thank you,' she said as soon as she went in.

'What for?' asked Mummy.

'My birthday present, the pram,' said Clare.

'Pram,' repeated Daddy, looking at Mummy. 'Do you know anything about a pram?'

Mummy smiled at Clare and said, 'Daddy's only teasing, darling. We hope you like it. Happy Birthday.'
Aren't birthdays lovely?

June 3

WHAT WILL I BE?

'What will I be when I grow up?'
Thought June one day, by a stream.
'Will I be pretty? Will I be rich?
'Oh, it's awfully nice to dream.'

'I could marry a king,
'And then I'd be queen,
'And wear silks and satins and jewels.
'And the people would say,
'I hope every day,
'How wisely our dear queen she rules.'

'Or I could be quite poor,
'And dressed in old rags,

'And live in a house, oh, so shabby.
'But what do I care how I will fare.
'As long as I'm blissfully happy?'

June 4

SARA HAD A FLOCK OF SHEEP

Sara had a flock of sheep
She loved each one a lot.
She called each one by its own name,
Peggy, Sue and Dot.

But sheep are really silly beasts,
And never called her Sara.
All they had to say to her,
Was 'Baa-baa, Baa-baa, Baa-baa.'

89

June 5

DAD'S PIG

Dad came home with a pig one night, but Mum told him that he couldn't keep it in our flat. There was no room.

Dad said he'd change it the next day and that night it slept under the bed and tried to eat the bedclothes. Mum was furious.

The next morning Dad took the pig away and came back with a piano. There was no room in our flat to keep a piano, and although I would have loved to learn to play it, Mum made him take it away the next morning.

He came back with some tickets.

'What are these?' asked Mum.

'I swapped the piano for some tickets for the theatre tonight. We're all going to a show.'

I was so excited when we set off, but after an hour in the theatre I was bored, and began to wish we'd kept the pig. Mum was sound asleep, and I think she probably agreed with me.

June 6

NATIONAL DAY

Miss Thompson said to her class one day, 'You all come from lots of different countries, so tomorrow I want you all to wear the costumes that you wear in your own countries.'

The next day Sun-Li wore a silk jacket and silk trousers, with little slits in the sides. 'This is what they wear in China,' she said. Mac wore a kilt and tweed jacket. 'I am from the Highlands of Scotland, and this is the Scottish costume,' he told the rest of the class.

Just then John came in. Everyone knew he was English, but he was wearing baggy pants and shoes with turned-up toes. On his head he wore a funny hat. He had a loose shirt on, too.

'John,' said Miss Thompson. 'We were expecting you in English clothes. You are English, after all.'

'I know, Miss,' he said, 'but my grand-dad was Turkish and I'm proud of that, so I thought I'd wear what they wear in Turkey.'

'Thank goodness he doesn't come from Lapland,' shouted Mac. 'It's much too hot to wear fur coats today.'

And everyone laughed.

June 7

THE MAGIC WHISTLE

There was once a princess who had been

given a magic whistle by her fairy god-mother. Whenever it was blown, any animal that heard it would come under the spell of the person who had had blown it.

The years passed and the princess fell in love with a poor shepherd, but since he was a shepherd her father, the king, would not allow her to marry him. 'You must marry a prince,' he said, but each one who came to ask for her hand was rejected by the princess.

Eventually the king became exasperated with his daughter. 'Very well,' he cried, 'you can marry whoever you choose as long as he fulfils one condition. He must round up and bring to me one thousand hares.'

When the shepherd heard this, he said, 'It is impossible.'

But the princess gave him her magic whistle and sent him into the fields. The shepherd blew it and as soon as the hares heard it, they fell under its spell. He had soon rounded up one thousand hares and walked with them into the palace courtyard. The king was aghast that such a humble lad was to be his son-in-law, but the shepherd was such a charming fellow that the king became very fond of him. And the princess and the shepherd lived happily ever after.

June 8

THE MICE AND THE CAT'S BELL

For many years the mice had been living in fear of their enemy, the cat. It was decided to call a meeting of all the mice to determine the best means of handling the situation. Many plans were discussed, but none of them was any good.

Eventually a young mouse got up and said, 'I propose that a bell be hung round the cat's neck. Then, whenever the cat approaches, we shall always hear him before he gets to us and we can run off.' All the mice voted on the resolution and it was passed by a huge majority.

But then an old mouse spoke. 'Friends,' he said, 'it takes a young mouse to think of so ingenious a plan. With a bell round the cat's neck we shall all be safe. But there is one little problem. Who is going to put the bell round the cat's neck?'

Silence fell. A few minutes later the meeting broke up with all the mice agreeing that it was a good idea if only it was workable.

June 9

THE MAGIC SHELL

Dan was a little boy who went one year

to the seaside for his holidays with his mother and father. He had a wonderful time. There was a swimming pool where he learned to swim, and a fun fair where he spent quite a lot of his holiday savings money.

He spent hours on the super beach making sandcastles and sandpies.

On the final day he went for a last walk along the shore. He was so sad to be going home again.

All of a sudden he saw a beautiful golden shell at his feet. He picked it up and put it in his pocket. When they arrived home he showed it to his parents. 'That's lucky, Dan,' said his mother. 'That's a dolphin shell. If you hold it to your ear you'll be able to hear the sound of the sea lapping against the shore.'

Dan did just that and it was true. Every time he wanted to hear the sea and remember his super holiday, he put the shell to his ear and there was the sound of the sea.

June 10

MISS IVY'S BIRDS

Miss Ivy was a very nice old lady who lived all alone apart from two pet birds that she had had for years and years. One bright sunny day she decided to go for a drive in her old car.

When she took the car out of the garage she looked up at the window and saw her two birds. She felt awfully sorry for them being cooped up inside on such a lovely day, so she went back into the house to them. 'I'll take you for a drive if you promise to stay in the car,' she said.

The two birds twittered their promise and off the three of them went—and do you know what? The birds behaved so well that Miss Ivy often took them out in her car whenever the sun shone brightly. And the birds loved her so much that they never once tried to fly away.

June 11

THE MAGIC COOKING POT

A young girl was once given a magic cooking pot by an old lady whom she helped one day. 'To make it cook all you have to say is "Pot, cook!" and to make it stop say, "Pot, stop!"', said the old lady.

The girl took the pot home to her mother, who was very poor and the two were never hungry again. Indeed there was so much food that the mother and daughter sold some of it and soon became quite wealthy and did not need to use the pot very often.

One day, a jealous neighbour happened to be passing by when the pot was being used. She heard the girl say, 'Pot, cook!' and was amazed when she saw what happened. So that night the neighbour stole the pot from the mother and her daughter.

She took it home and said the magic words and the pot began to cook. Soon there was enough porridge, but the thief had no idea how to make it stop. After a few minutes there was porridge everywhere — it flowed out of the kitchen, into the street. The true owners of the pot were awakened by their neighbour's screams for help and ran to tell the pot to stop cooking.

From then on the pot was kept under lock and key and the neighbour was so ashamed of being branded a robber that she left the district soon afterwards and was never seen again.

June 12

TINA AND TIM

It was Tina's birthday and her friend Tim had been practising singing 'Happy Birthday to You' for weeks so that he could sing it to Tina when he gave her her birthday present. But, oh dear, when he wakened up he had a dreadfully sore throat and could not sing.

He went to Tina's house with her birthday flowers and tried to explain that he could not sing, when suddenly his pet canary flew down and landed on his peaked cap. He had heard Tim practise so often that he knew the words perfectly, and when Tim gave Tina her

present, the bird sang 'Happy Birthday, Dear Tina' perfectly.

It was the nicest birthday Tina had ever had.

June 13

FREDDY AND THE BICYCLE

When Freddy was given his first bicycle, he immediately began to learn how to ride it. In a couple of days he was perfect at it—so good that he thought he would teach his dog to ride it.

He sat the dog on the ground and showed him how to keep his front paws in the right position and how to pedal with his back legs. The dog seemed to be getting quite good at it, so Freddy sat him on the saddle; but as soon as he let go, the bicycle fell over right on top of a cat. 'What do you think you're doing?' asked the cat.

'Learning to ride the bicycle,' said the dog.

'Why? Does Freddy play with your rubber bone and does he run after sticks when his father throws them?' the cat went on.

'No, he doesn't.'

'Well, why should you learn to ride his bike?' asked the cat.

The dog couldn't think of an answer and that was the last lesson he ever allowed himself to be given.

June 14

THE OLD WOMAN AND HER MAIDS

A thrifty old woman kept two serving maids to help with her housework. The two maids slept together in the loft and the lady used to rouse them at cockcrow.

Naturally the maidservants disliked very much being wakened before daylight every morning. They decided that if they could prevent the cock crowing, they would be able to stay longer in bed. So they strangled the cock.

But the old lady was so afraid of oversleeping that she took to rising at midnight every night from then on.

The girls had to obey her and were soon sorry that they had killed the cockerel. But, as they said to each other, too much cunning often overreaches itself.

***

June 15

THE CAT AND THE BICYCLE

Remember Freddy and the bicycle? He had a friend called Mike, who also had a bike.

One day, Mike came round for Freddy and Freddy was amazed to see that he had brought his cat with him.

'Does your cat like cycling?' he asked Mike.

'He loves it. Why don't you bring your cat out for a ride?'

So Freddy went and picked up the cat

and sat him on his shoulders as he rode out with Mike on his bike.

When they all got home, the dog growled at the cat, 'I thought you thought it was silly to ride bikes.'

'It is really, but it was great fun. I hope he takes me out again.'

'Life is not fair,' complained the dog.

'Oh well. It's a dog's life, isn't it?' said the cat and ran off.

June 16

SILLY DOG

Young Tony was on his way to meet his sister Mary, on her way back from school. 'Take the dog with you,' his mother had said.

When they got to the main road, the dog saw Mary at the other side and barked excitedly. He was a strong dog and was so keen to get to Mary that he pulled Tony right off the pavement as he tried to get to her.

All the cars came to a sudden halt, because the silly dog had not bothered to check if the green man was showing. 'You must look and listen and wait until the green man is showing before you cross the road,' said Mary; and from that day on the dog did just that.

June 17

CELIA LEARNS A LESSON

Celia had been given a lovely white kitten and a new doll with brown hair and green eyes for her birthday.

But Celia was a great tease. She dangled playthings above her kitten's head and laughed as it stretched to get them. But she never did let it get the toys to play with. Sometimes she held its front paws and made it dance with her.

It was the same with the doll. It lay unloved in a corner.

'I'm going to teach Celia a lesson,' said her mother one night. She took the kitten and the doll round to Celia's grandmother's house and asked her to look after them for a day or two. When Celia got up the next morning, her mother told her that the kitten and the doll had run away to find a kinder mistress. Celia cried and said that if they did come back she would take great care of them.

After two days the cat and the doll came back and Celia kept her promise and loved them both dearly.

June 18

THE FEARLESS KNIGHT

One day, a fearless knight rode into a town which was completely deserted. There was absolutely no sign of anyone. The knight suddenly stopped dead in his tracks, for there, in the path ahead, stood the most fearsome dragon. It had three horrible heads, and fire breathed out of each of its three mouths.

'It is no wonder that the town is deserted,' thought the knight. 'All the people are hiding from this beast.'

Without thinking of his own safety, he charged at the dragon, but the heat from its fire was such that he had to retreat.

Just then it started to rain and the dragon's flames were put out by the large raindrops. The brave knight charged again and this time his lance struck true and hard. A few seconds later the dragon lay dead. The knight cut its vicious heads off and carried them back to town. 'The dragon is dead,' he cried. A few minutes later the people came out from their houses. They begged their hero to stay with them, but the knight refused. 'There are other dragons and other people to help.' And off he rode seeking new adventures.

June 19

THE MAN WITH TWO WIVES

There was a time when men were allowed to have two wives, and there was once a middle-aged man, whose hair was just beginning to turn grey, who fell in love with two women and married them both.

One was young and lovely and wished her husband to be as youthful looking as herself, so every night she combed his hair and pulled out all the grey hairs.

The other woman was much older and approved of her husband's grey hair, for it made him look as old as she was. So every morning she would brush his hair and pick out some of the black hairs she found.

For a time the man enjoyed the attention of both his brides, until he looked in the mirror one morning and found he was completely bald.

Oh well, if you give in to everyone's wishes all the time, you will soon have nothing left to give.

June 20

THE HEDGEHOG AND THE DOG

A hedgehog once met a boastful dog. 'I am much faster than you,' said the dog. 'I am the fastest animal in the world.'

The hedgehog soon grew tired of the dog's boasting and challenged him to a race. 'Tomorrow, you race at this side of the hedgerow and I'll race at the other,' said the hedgehog.

The next day at noon the race began. The dog was half way up his side of the hedgerow when the hedgehog popped his head round at the other end and said, 'Not finished the first length yet?'

The dog got to the end of the hedgerow and turned round, but he was less than halfway down when the same thing happened.

The dog was so dispirited that he gave up and went home.

Now hedgehogs cannot run as fast as dogs — so can you guess what the clever hedgehog had done? He had told his wife, who looked exactly the same as him, to stand at the other end of the hedgerow to himself and pretend to be him. The clever hedgehog did not move at all, but the dog thought that he had run much faster than he had. It served him right for being so boastful, didn't it?

The terrified man did as he was told and within a few minutes the yard had been swept until it was quite spotless.

I wonder if it could have been the smith's wife in disguise. If it wasn't, well, maybe it was a witch!

June 22

THE THREE CHICKENS

'My eggs are bigger than yours,' boasted a chicken one day.

'Rubbish,' said a second chicken.

'Mine are much bigger than yours,' cried a third.

Just then the cockerel came over and asked what all the noise was about. When he found out he said, 'Very well. You must all go to the coop and lay one egg each. Whichever lays the largest will be the winner.'

The three birds went off and a few

June 21

THE BLACKSMITH AND THE WITCH

In some parts of the world, people believe that on Midsummer's Eve witches leave their houses and play tricks.

A blacksmith once left the tavern where he had been drinking with his friends although he had promised that he would sweep the yard for his wife.

He must have drunk a little too much, for, as he made his way home, he seemed to hear witches' hollow laughter all around.

It was a great relief when he saw the lights of the smithy ahead of him, but when he went into the yard, there stood a hideous witch. She ran towards him and pushed her broom into his hands. 'Sweep this yard spotless or else I shall carry you off to be my slave forever,' the witch commanded the smith.

99

minutes later came back clutching their eggs. They were all about the same size, but the cockerel decided to weigh them to see which was the biggest. Along came a turkey and looked at the three eggs. 'What puny little eggs,' it crowed. And having said that, it immediately laid a huge egg that put the chickens' eggs quite to shame.

'Much too big,' said the first chicken.

'Vulgar thing,' cried the second.

'What does size matter?' asked the third.

'Exactly,' agreed the other two and the three went off for lunch.

June 23

THE TWO SISTERS

One day a young girl went into the woods to pick some wild strawberries. She searched and searched but could not find one single berry. As she sat and ate her lunch a little ant came up to her and asked her for a crumb. 'Go away,' said the girl. 'I have only enough for me.'

The next day her younger sister went to find some berries and returned a few hours later with a basket full of beautiful, plump fruit.

'Where did you find those?' asked her sister.

'I couldn't find any at first,' said the girl. 'But when I was having lunch a little ant passed by and asked me for a morsel. I gave it half of what I had and it was so grateful that it led me to a secret place which was full of the most beautiful strawberries.'

Generosity can pay the most unexpected dividends.

June 24

THE TWO BARRELS

Two barrels there were
Who didn't have hair.
And they loathed being called
The two barrels bald.

Said one to the other,
'Do you know what, my brother?
Let's go ask the vats
If they'll lend us two hats.'

So that's just what they did
They borrowed two lids,
And now, willy nilly
They're the two barrels silly.

June 25

JUDE AND THE ANTS

One evening Jude set off with his horse

THE FOX AND THE GEESE

A fox came into a meadow one day where there was a fine flock of geese quietly grazing. He looked at them and began to lick his lips. 'This is my lucky day. I shall eat them all for my supper,' he said to himself.

The geese began to honk in fear and then one young goose said, 'If we must die at least let us sing one last song.'

'I am in no hurry for my supper,' said the fox. 'Go ahead.'

The first goose began to sing, and was soon joined by the second and the third and soon all the geese were singing the same song. The fox didn't know that it was a song of crying for help, but the goosegirl who was in the next field recognized the song, and ran to the field to chase the fox away.

'Next time I'm faced with such a chance as that,' said the fox as he ran off, 'I won't waste time. I'll always grab every opportunity from now on.'

---

to see his grandmother. At the edge of the woods he came across the embers of a fire. The flames were beginning to spread and were threatening to destroy an ant hill.

Jude immediately doused them, and was surprised when one of the ants from the hill came up to him and said, 'Thank you, Jude. One good turn deserves another. We will help you one day.'

Jude arrived at his grandmother's house later that evening to find the old lady in a great state of excitement. 'Jude,' she cried, 'a fox was just about to steal one of my lambs when suddenly a crowd of ants appeared and drove the fox off. And after the fox had gone, the ants said that they had helped me because you had helped them, and they were returning the favour.'

Jude was never sceptical of the ants' powers again. He had forgotten that a lot of tiny things, if joined together, can become a powerful force.

CHINESE WHISPERS

Two cats were enjoying a nap one day when they were awakened by a little mouse. 'Don't tell anyone but the farmer's wife's in red,' it said.

'What was that?' asked one of the cats.

'The farmer's wife's in bed.'

A few minutes later a flock of geese passed by.

'Don't tell anyone,' said the second cat, 'but the farmer's wife is dead.'

News soon spread around the farm and all the animals were so sad that they picked a bunch of flowers for the farmer.

They were astonished when the farmer's wife came to the door wearing

a lovely red dress. 'How nice,' she cried. 'They match my new dress exactly. It's a surprise for the farmer. It's our wedding anniversary and I was wearing a dress like this on the night we met.'

June 28

THE PEARL NECKLACE

A peasant's son was on his way to market one day. As he passed the royal palace he saw a pearl necklace lying in the grass.

'One of the princesses must have dropped it,' he said to himself, and took it to the king.

'Such honesty must be rewarded,' said the king.

'I want nothing more than the honour of placing it on the neck of the owner,' said the lad.

The king called his three daughters to the throne room, but none of them had lost the necklace. Just then the queen herself came into the throne room. 'Ah!' she exclaimed. 'My necklace.'

The boy put the necklace around the queen's neck and as he did so the king began to laugh.

'I was going to offer the lad the hand of whichever of our daughters had lost the necklace. It's just as well I didn't, isn't it?'

June 29

THE COW AND THE OX

There was once a young cow who never having felt the yoke spent all her time in the fields as free as free could be. One day she went up to the ox who worked hard for his living.

'How foolish you are,' the cow said. 'Why work all day long. Come and play with me, it's much better fun, I assure you.'

'How do you feel now? You must know now why you were allowed to live your life of idleness for so long. I would much rather feel the weight of the yoke, than the cut of the knife.'

It's quite true that he that laughs best laughs last, isn't it?

June 30

THE SEAL FAMILY

A family of seals once lived happily together. One day the father seal found three sailors' hats in the water. He put the largest one on his own head and to his joy it fitted perfectly. The smaller two fitted both his sons perfectly, and Mother Seal was very proud of her menfolk as they swam around in their hats.

After a few days, Father Seal said to the boys, 'It's Mummy's birthday tomorrow, what shall we buy her?'

The old ox said nothing but went on with his work. When evening came he was turned loose by the farmer and went to the village. When he arrived there, he saw that the fine young cow was about to be offered as sacrifice.

The ox went up to the cow and said,

'A new apron,' suggested the older son.

'A new brush,' suggested the second.

'I don't think she'd like any of those,' said Daddy Seal.

'I know,' cried both the young seals together. 'She's only got her old head-scarf to wear. Let's buy her a sailor's hat, too.'

And that's just what they did; and Mummy Seal loved her sailor's hat and wore it as often as her husband and sons wore theirs.

July 1

THE LIZARD AND THE TORTOISE

There was once a little green lizard who loved to lie in the sun among the rocks. One fine and sunny day she crawled up on a tortoise's horny back, thinking it was a pile of stones. She lay down and fell fast asleep. And as she slept, she did not even notice that the pile of stones began to move.

Who knows where the tortoise would have taken the little lizard, if he had not stumbled on the way across the ditch. The lizard woke up. 'Goodness!' she cried. 'Where are the stones taking me?' The astonished tortoise stopped, and asked who was speaking, since he could not feel the lizard on his back.

'Stones? What stones? I'm a tortoise!' he cried, and the lizard jumped off and hurried home. It wasn't far. We all know how slowly tortoises walk.

July 2

HOW MICHAEL FELL INTO A TREE

Michael had come to spend the holidays with his grandmother. The day after he had arrived he set off for the fishpond.

But as soon as he lay down on the bank above the water, the ground seemed to give way beneath him, and he went rolling down towards the water like a runaway marble. Luckily, there was a tree growing right out of the bottom of the fishpond and Michael headed straight for it. He caught hold of a branch and there he was, sprawled across its crown.

hat.' And the green snake cried out, 'That's good, because I like the pink one better.'

And when their bewildered father explained that it was meant to be the other way round, the pink snake told him, 'Because I am always looking at my green brother here, I supposed that I, too, was green.' And the green snake said, 'And as I see only my pink brother, I thought I was pink!' Their father sighed to himself. 'Dear me,' he said, 'what a pity I didn't buy you a mirror in town.'

July 4

THE TWO FISHERMEN

On the bank of a fishpond, two fishermen were arguing about who had caught a small carp. After a while they had come to blows over the skinny little fish.

'It's mine. I pulled it out,' cried the first.

'It's mine. It was in my net,' shouted the second.

'Well, well,' he thought to himself, 'many's the time I've fallen out of a tree, but this is the first time I've ever fallen into one!'

He looked around him, and in the ditch below the bank he saw some village boys. They had just put the plank back across the gap at the top of the dike, and were covering it with sods. Then they hid in the ditch and waited for another unsuspecting lad to come and lie down on the plank just like Michael had a moment earlier.

July 3

THE PINK SNAKE AND THE GREEN SNAKE

Once upon a time there were two snakes. One of them was pink from head to tail, while the other was green. Their father bought them both little hats; a pink one for the pink snake and a green one for the green.

When he came back from town and gave the snakes their hats, the pink snake said, 'Father, I want the green

Just then Mat, the son of a blacksmith in the village, happened to pass by. He saw the fishermen wrestling with each other, ignoring the half-dead fish that lay at their feet. He went up to them and threw the little fish back in the water.

'It doesn't belong to either of you,' he said. 'It still belongs in the water. Come back next year, when it has grown.'

So the fishermen decided to come back and try their luck next year.

July 5

SIMON AND GRANDFATHER'S MAGNIFYING GLASS

One day in the holidays, it was raining outside and Simon could not go swimming as usual. He was rummaging about among the old magazines and books in the attic. Inside one thick volume he came across a cloth case. When he opened it he found his grandfather's old magnifying glass inside.

Simon put it to his eye. 'Well, I never,' he said to himself. 'The world was really huge in grandfather's day. How terrifying.'

Before his eyes an enormous net stretched from beam to beam. In it sat a spider the size of a football. It goggled at Simon with eyes like a pair of tennis balls. A mouse which dashed across the attic floor and disappeared into a hole beneath the rafters seemed to him to be bigger than a tomcat.

'Everything must have been much, much bigger then,' thought Simon to himself. As the rain drummed on the roof, Simon dropped off to sleep and he

thought about how much nicer the little world of today is, now it had shrunk so much.

July 6

THE CLEVER COOK

Once upon a time a king heard from his wise men about the magic powers possessed by the meat of a certain green snake. It was said that whoever ate a little of this wonderful meat would hear everything that was being said, even if it were whispered behind closed doors. He would even be able to understand the twittering of the birds, the conversation of animals, and the buzzing of insects.

The king ordered his cook to roast him some of this snake meat. But the sly

cook roasted an eel along with the snake. He served this to the king, and ate the snake himself.

He had no sooner finished his unusual meal, than a fly went buzzing past, saying, 'The king has secretly imprisoned the daughter of King John of Strandal. Set her free, and King John will reward you well.'

The cook released the princess that very night and was given her hand in marriage by King John, as well as half the kingdom.

July 7

HOW MAT PASTURED DEER

One day, Mat the blacksmith's son was sitting on the riverbank. As he watched the water flowing slowly by, he thought to himself how splendid it would be to be able to float along with it. The moment he had thought this, the little carp he had thrown back into the fishpond not very long ago popped out of the water.

'How did you get here?' Mat asked him in surprise.

'Pond or river, it's the same water everywhere,' said the carp. 'You wanted to float along with the water; well, here's a boat for you.' Mat clambered into it, and before very long he drifted along to a beautiful castle. He liked the place so much that he asked the king to employ him as a shepherd. But the king kept deer, not sheep, and there were just a hundred of them. Mat drove them down to the river, but they ran off in all directions. 'However am I going to find them?' he sighed to himself.

At that moment the carp appeared and gave Mat a reed whistle. When he blew it all the deer came running back, and spent the rest of the day grazing by the riverside.

July 8

JIMMY AND THE PLOPPER

Jimmy climbed into a willow tree whose branches hung over the fishpond. It made a good spot from which to jump into the water.

Jimmy was just thinking what a lovely splash he would make if he jumped in, when he noticed, on the same branch but a little higher up, a strange-looking creature. It was half fish, half bird, and was green all over.

'What on earth are you?' Jimmy asked.

107

'Why, a Plopper, of course,' replied the fish-bird, or bird-fish, grumpily. 'I spend all day and all night plopping into the water, and you have no idea how tired I am! Do you think you might plop for me today, so that I might take a rest?'

Jimmy said he would love to, and spent that whole day, right until the sun set, doing the plopping for the Plopper!

July **9**

WHY FROGS CROAK

The stork, king of the frogs, decreed one day that all frogs were forbidden to quack out loud.

'Who could put up with all that

noise?' he said. 'Your endless chatter is giving me a headache!' But the frogs, especially the gossipy old dears among them, soon found a way to get the better of the stork. Since they weren't allowed to quack any more, they invented a special sign language. They began to talk to each other using their hands and fingers—a new language.

Their king didn't understand a word of it, which didn't suit him at all, of course. So he quickly made a new proclamation that all frogs must croak. Ever since then they have croaked, but when they want to tell each other something they don't want the stork to know, they remember to use the frog sign language again.

July **10**

DAN MEETS THE DOLPHIN

One summer, when Dan arrived at the seaside for the holidays, and unpacked his diving gear on the beach—goggles and a pair of flippers—he turned to his father with a look of disappointment, and said, 'Where's my oxygen cylinder?'

His father smiled, and told him it would be a few years yet before he could have one of those.

'You know I wanted to dive to the very bottom of the sea this year, and visit the dolphin, and . . .'

'Why should you go diving to the bottom of the sea? That can wait until you're older. There's the dolphin over there,' said Dan's father and he pointed to the sea.

There was a fine surf up, and on the crest of one of the white waves, the dolphin came swimming onto the beach. How glad the dolphin was to see Dan. The two played together all day until it was time for bed.

July 11

THE HAMSTER AND THE FIELDMICE

'Good neighbour,' said the fieldmouse to the hamster one day, 'the harvest is just around the corner. Why do we not join forces this year? You could harvest the ears of wheat, and my family and I will take out the grains. Then we shall take equal shares.'

'Why not,' said the hamster. 'At least the work will be done more quickly.'

So the hamster brought in the ears, the fieldmice took out the grains, and then they divided them into five piles. The first pile was for Father Fieldmouse, the second for Mother Fieldmouse, one each for the fieldmouse children, and only the fifth for the hamster.

'If I am to get only every fifth grain,' said the hamster, 'then you shall have every fifth ear.'

And that's what happened.

Since then the hamster has never shared the work at harvest time, but has minded his own business.

July 12

THE MICE GO FOR A WALK

One Sunday afternoon the mice were getting ready to take their Sunday walk. They were all dressed up in their Sunday best when they suddenly found they couldn't find the key to the front door.

'You were the last to lock up,' said the first mouse. 'You must remember where you put the key.'

'On the nail, where it always hangs,' retorted the second. 'Where else would I put it?'

'You've probably left it in the lock,' said the first mouse. And that's exactly where the silly mouse found it.

July 13

THE STORK AND THE GREEN FROG

On the bank of a lake a little green frog met a stork. She was so terrified of his tall legs and his ever-so-long neck and beak, that for a while she couldn't even manage to croak. But when she had recovered herself, she said to the stork, 'Good day,' and asked him, since he was so tall, to take a look across to the other side of the lake.

'You see, sir, I am expecting visitors. My two aunts and all my cousins are coming.'

And she went on to tell him how plump and well-fed they all were, since there had always been much more of everything over there on the opposite bank.

'I'm glad to hear it,' said the stork, who was quite peckish. He turned his head to take a look to see if the fat little frogs were on their way. That was just what the little frog was waiting for, and with a splash she disappeared into the lake.

NEIGHBOUR MATTHEW AND NEIGHBOUR JOHN

Matthew was on his way to visit his neighbour John. On the doorstep he met John's son Joseph.

'What's your Dad doing, Joseph?' he asked.

'He was just going to have his lunch, but when he saw you through the window he hid the goose in the oven, the ham behind the stove and the buns on the shelf.'

Matthew went into the house, and his neighbour greeted him, saying, 'Pity you didn't come sooner, neighbour, we might have had lunch together.'

'I couldn't come sooner,' Matthew replied. 'I met something very strange on the way. It was a snake with a head as big as the ham you have behind the stove, as fat as the goose in the oven, and all brown and white like the buns over there on the shelf.'

John was so ashamed of himself that he took the food from hiding-places and asked Matthew to stay to lunch.

July 15

MAT THE HAREHERD

The last time we came across Mat was when he had to pasture a hundred deer, and the carp lent him a hand. That evening, when he drove them all back to the castle, the king frowned and said, 'Tomorrow you shall have a hundred hares to look after, and if a single one is

a loud *bang!* He grabbed his paw, for something had started to prick it as though he had a thorn there. He left his pasture and hobbled off home where he would put a poultice on his paw and by morning it would be all right again. But when he woke up the next day his whole leg was swollen, and he couldn't run at all.

So he put on his best clothes and limped along to the doctor. The woodpecker doctor examined the leg and shook his head. 'A fine thorn, that one,' he said. 'Look what you had in your paw.' He showed the hare a piece of lead shot. The hare thanked the doctor for curing him, and went back home in high spirits.

July 17

THE FOX AND THE GOAT

A fox and a goat met one summer's day. They were both very hot and thirsty.

'Why should we be so uncomfortable?' said the fox. 'Why don't we jump into the well?'

The goat liked the idea, so they jumped into the well. When they had drunk their fill, the goat asked, 'But how do we get out again?'

'I'll tell you how,' said the fox. 'Stand on your hind legs, rest your horns on the side of the well, and I shall climb out over your back. When I get out, I shall help you up.'

'Good idea,' said the goat, and he did as the fox had suggested. The fox clambered out quickly, and that was the last the goat saw of him. Fortunately the

missing when you return in the evening, you will lose your head.'

The next day Mat drove the hares down to the meadow by the river, and they ran off even more quickly than the deer had done. He could already see himself being led off to the executioner, hands tied behind his back. Then he remembered the reed whistle in his pocket. He tried blowing it, to see whether it worked for hares, too. It did, and all at once the hares came running back again, and started to graze like sheep.

July 16

THE HARE AND DOCTOR WOODPECKER

A hare was feeding near the bushes on the meadow bank where the thorns are needle-sharp, when he suddenly heard

farmer passed just then and helped the goat out, or else he would have been stuck there forever.

July 18

HASSAN AND OLD FOUR-EYES

Whenever little Hassan started to play his pipe, Old Four-eyes, his snake, raised his funny big head and started twisting and turning it about. He waved the rest of his body around, too, in time with Hassan's tune, as if marking time for the piper. That's why they called him Four-eyes the conductor.

'Hassan,' said the old snake one day, 'I find all this conducting very tiring these days. Either I'm poorly, or I'm getting old.'

'But how are we to earn a living?' asked Hassan.

'I'll tell you what,' said Old Four-eyes, 'we'll swap over. I'll play the pipe, and you'll do the conducting.'

113

What a sight THAT was, once they had got it right!

Money from the passers-by simply rained down at their feet.

July 19

HOW MONKEYS PLAY HIDE-AND-SEEK

The little black boy and his friend the monkey liked playing hide-and-seek. One day the boy hid so deep in the undergrowth that he was afraid he wouldn't be able to find his way out again. He curled up among the leaves and listened quietly for the sound of footsteps or the rustle of branches nearby. But he heard nothing but the sound of his own heart, beating excitedly in his breast.

'Why doesn't the monkey look for me? Why doesn't he call out to me?' he thought. Then he looked up towards the treetops. And there was the monkey sitting on a branch, grinning down at him. The little boy called up to him, thinking to himself how difficult it is to hide from a monkey who can swing through the trees.

July 20

THE WOLF AND THE STORK

A greedy wolf swallowed a bone one day while he was having his lunch. It got stuck deep in his throat and although he tried to pull it out, he couldn't get at it with his paw.

A stork happened to be passing by, and the wolf asked him to help.

'Why are you so greedy, wolf?' the stork chided him, pulling the bone out with his long beak.

The stork thought the wolf would be grateful, but when he said nothing at all, the bird said, 'You might at least say thank-you.'

'*I* — thank *you*?' asked the wolf, surprised. 'It should be you who thanks me. After all, who else can say he had his head right between my jaws, and came to no harm?'

July 21

ARIF AND THE CONDOR

Little Arif-Omar was the only one to survive when his caravan became lost among the desert sand-dunes. He was found by a condor, who carried him off to the nest and set him down among the little condors.

And there Arif stayed until he had grown into a sturdy young lad. One day the condor decided it was time for him

to learn to fly. He shoved the boy out of the nest, as he had done with the rest of his brood, but Arif just flapped his arms and fell deep into the sand.

'You shall sleep down there on the sand tonight, to teach you a lesson,' the condor told him. But how surprised he was when Arif climbed like a squirrel back into the nest, snuggled among his warm feathers, and fell fast asleep.

THE VIZIER AND THE MIRAGE

A vizier set off on his camel to ride round some of the Sultan's land which had been entrusted to his care. But he got lost in the desert, and to make matters worse he ran out of water. After a short while both he and his camel were half dead with thirst.

Several times he thought he saw a lush green oasis ahead of him, but when he drew closer it always turned out to be a mirage.

He was disappointed so many times, that when he finally did come to an oasis, he didn't believe his eyes, thinking it was another mirage. Even when they drew him a jug of water from the spring, he didn't believe it was all true. It was only when the water touched his lips and he swallowed the first cool mouthful that he sighed at last with relief: Allah be praised . . .

called down, 'Now you have the whole cheese to yourself!' And he ran off as quickly as possible.

July 23

THE MOON, THE FOX AND THE WOLF

Early one evening a fox saw the moon in the well. He thought it was a cheese, and since his stomach was rumbling with hunger, without hesitation he leaped into the bucket. When he got to the bottom, he found out he had been mistaken; it had only been a reflection in the water. How was he to get out again?

Just then a wolf passed by the well. 'Friend wolf, might I invite you to share my excellent cheese? If you want some, just take hold of the end of the rope and let yourself down,' the fox called out.

The wolf took hold of the rope, and as he went down into the well he pulled up the fox in the bucket with his weight. When he was safely at the top, the fox

---

July 24

THE ONE-HUMPED CAMEL AND THE TWO-HUMPED CAMEL

One morning a camel driver woke up both his animals and began to put on their harnesses, halters and reins.

As usual, he started with the one-humped camel. As he was passing the halter over the animal's head, the camel asked him why he must always be the first one up, while the two-humped camel was still lying asleep in the sand.

'Well, I take you in order of humps,' said the camel driver. 'First the one-humped camel, then the two-humped. And if I had a three-humped camel, he would be third.'

But in the end he decided it really was

unfair that the one-humped camel was first to be awakened, and the next day he woke the two-humped camel first.

July 25

HOW THE WOLF DRESSED UP AS A SHEPHERD

One day a wolf dressed himself up as a shepherd. He had found a sheepskin coat and hat. He even made himself a crook from a branch he almost tripped over in the forest. From a distance he looked almost like any other shepherd working in the fields.

So disguised, and leaning on his crook with his front paws, the wolf crept up that evening to the flock of sheep. But, of course, as soon as he tried to speak he gave himself away. Instead of words, only growls came out. Even the wolf himself got a surprise, because he thought that if he looked like a shepherd, he would also sound like one. So he tripped over his crook and it was the easiest thing in the world for the real shepherd and his dog to catch him and drive him far away.

July 26

THE TAILOR AND THE PEASANT

A tailor once set out into the world to seek his fortune. He packed his worldly goods into a bundle, and off he went.

On the way he met a peasant who was taking a hare to market in a sack.

'A hare might come in handy,' the tailor said to himself, and he gave the peasant his bundle in return for the creature.

After a while he came to a village where a number of linden trees grew. Now, the tailor had heard somewhere that a whip made of linden bast would drive off the devil himself, so he stopped to peel off some of the bark, and plaited himself a whip.

Now, you may ask what all this has to do with the picture. You will have to wait until tomorrow to find out, because I am going off to bed now and you should too.

July 27

THE TAILOR AND THE THREE PRINCESSES

That evening the tailor arrived in a deep

forest. There a black cart drawn by black horses drove up. Out of the cart stepped a princess, who was dressed all in black. 'Well, Satan, here I am,' she said. 'Take me where you have taken my two sisters.'

The tailor hardly had time to explain that he was not the devil, but a tailor, before the real devil appeared.

The tailor told the fiend he would not get the princess, and struck him with his whip of linden. Then he added, 'If you wish to be spared further blows, bring back the princess's sisters this minute.'

The devil ran off and the princess explained to the tailor that the devil had captured her two sisters, and she missed them so much that her father had sadly agreed that she should join them.

When the sisters were united once more, the tailor took them all back to their father, who rewarded him well and held a huge banquet in his honour.

July 28
HOW THE DOVE AND THE ANT HELPED EACH OTHER

A dove once alighted beside a clear mountain stream in order to drink some water. Some distance away an ant was also drinking from the stream. As it bent over, it fell into the water, and was unable to get back to the bank.

The dove hurried over to help it. She laid a straw across the water and pushed it towards the drowning ant. The ant crawled along it to safety.

Before the ant could say anything, along came a hunter, and drew his bow to shoot the dove. As he was about to loose his arrow, the ant bit him in the heel and before he had recovered himself, the dove had flown away.

One good turn deserves another.

July 29
HOW THE BLACK BOY KEPT HIS WORD

A black boy once wanted to get to his grandmother's as quickly as possible, for he was to spend the holidays there. He asked the ostrich, who was famous for his swift running, to take him.

'Why not?' replied the ostrich, 'if you can manage to hold on.'

The little black boy waved his hand,

as if to say that it was the easiest thing in the world, and climbed onto the ostrich's back. But as soon as the big bird started running, the lad fell into the sand like a pear from a tree.

'That was only the first time,' said the boy, and he climbed up on the ostrich's back a second time. The ostrich asked how many more times he wanted to fall.

'Only once more — into Granny's arms,' said the little black boy, and so the ostrich carried him safely there.

July 30
THE FOX AND THE GRAPES

A fox was once passing by a vineyard, and his stomach was rumbling with hunger. High up above him, he saw bunches of beautiful grapes hanging in the sunshine.

The fox licked his lips greedily, his mouth watering at the thought of the sweet breakfast he was to have.

He jumped up once, twice, a third time; but when he saw that he couldn't reach the grapes, he said to himself, 'Anyway, they are sour. I could pick such grapes anytime I wanted, but I don't like them one little bit!'

Some people do like to fool themselves, don't they?

The little black boy had a grand time at his grandmother's during the holidays. If he wanted some dates, all he had to do was go out into the garden and pick some. If he wanted to have an orange, he did the same. And there were pineapples and bananas everywhere!

But some of the trees were too tall for the young lad to climb. How was he to get up there?

Just then a giraffe passed by. The boy asked the giraffe to stand beside the orange tree and he climbed up its neck to the highest branches where the biggest and sweetest of the oranges were.

Late one evening, when the moon had slipped behind the clouds and it was as black as pitch, a bat felt like having a chat with someone.

He knocked on the weasel's door, but when she came to open it, the weasel shouted at him, 'Be off with you, mouse!'

'Who are you calling a mouse?' the bat cried. 'Can't you see I've got wings — can't you see I'm a bird?'

But the weasel slammed the door in his face, so the bat tried the hedgehog next door. As soon as the hedgehog saw him, he told him, 'Go away, I don't want anything to do with you, furry bird!'

'I'm no bird, hedgehog,' said the bat. 'You can see very well that I'm just a mouse.' But the hedgehog was not listening any more, and the sad little bat flew over the fishpond all alone, wishing he could be one thing or the other.

THE KNIGHT WITH THE WONDERFUL SWORD

Once upon a time there was a land that was in terror of a many-headed dragon. One day, a knight with a wonderful sword arrived at the palace and when the king told him of the trouble that the dragon was causing the knight laughed and said, 'How much worse it would be if he only had one head — a wise one.'

'They say that two heads are better than one,' he went on, 'but can you imagine, Your Majesty, what would happen to your kingdom if it was to be ruled by two heads rather than one? One would laugh and the other cry — and that would be the end of your kingdom.'

'True,' said the king. 'I will take you to the dragon's lair.' All the courtiers rode off with them. When they got there, the knight drew his wonderful sword. 'Off with the dragon's heads,' he cried. The sword cut through the dragon's heads and the beast lay dead at the knight's feet. But the sword had not known when to stop and beheaded several of the courtiers.

I'll tell you what happened tomorrow.

August 3
WHAT HAPPENED TO THE KNIGHT WITH THE WONDERFUL SWORD

When the knight with the wonderful sword had put paid to the dragon with the many heads and had also killed several of the courtiers, the king was so angry that he locked him in the tower.

The royal magician was summoned to sprinkle the water of life on the dead courtiers, but just as he had finished, he tripped and some of the water landed on the dragon, who came back to life.

'I demand a sacrifice,' he roared. 'Bring me the princess.'

The frightened king stammered that the princess would have to be suitably dressed and that if he would wait a few moments, he would arrange for the princess to be sent to him. He called his most trusted servant, told him loudly to bring the princess, and whispered to him to free the knight with the wonderful sword from the tower.

August 4
THE END OF THE MANY-HEADED DRAGON

The king led his daughter to the dragon as slowly as possible, praying that the knight would soon be released. But his courtiers thought that his wonderful

sword might execute them again, and so they exchanged his sword for another.

The knight came to the dragon's lair and drew what he thought was his wonderful sword. As soon as the dragon saw it, he assumed that the knight would behead him again, so he freed the princess and promised to leave the land for ever.

It was only when the dragon had gone and the princess was safely at home that the knight realized that his sword had been stolen. The king was furious and demanded that the guilty courtiers be brought before him. He ordered that all the men before him be beheaded. The knight and the princess had fallen in love and were married shortly after.

THE SUN-KING AND PRINCESS IWANTA

Princess Iwanta would not take no for an answer. Whenever she took a fancy to something, she had to have it at once. One day she asked the Sun-King to take her for a ride in his chariot.

The Sun-King, who knew Iwanta only too well, simply nodded his head, so the princess climbed aboard, and off they went. Or rather, off they flew, for the sun-chariot soared straight up over the clouds.

'That was a lovely little mountain valley we just flew over,' shouted Iwanta. 'Take me back to it!'

'You can have another look tomorrow,' said the king.

In vain did Iwanta stamp her feet, but they just flew on and on for days and days and days, until at last the princess promised the Sun-King she would never be wicked and haughty again.

August 6
THE HORSE AND THE DONKEY

One night, two robbers broke into a rich peasant's farm. They took everything they thought worth stealing, including a horse and a donkey. In their haste they loaded the whole of their spoils onto the donkey.

On the way to the forest the donkey began to stagger under the weight, and begged the horse to take half the burden. The horse refused. It was only when the donkey dropped down dead that the horse realized how foolish he had been not to help his long-eared companion.

The robbers loaded everything onto the horse's back, the donkey's skin as well, so his load was even more than the donkey's when it could so easily have been half.

August 7
A PRESENT FROM THE FAIR

Today there is a fair in our village; it's so big it's in two fields. A roundabout stands on the village green, along with some swings and a shooting gallery. Then there are stalls with sugar-candy, chocolate, sweets, nougat, gingerbread and marzipan. And, best of all, a candy-floss man. And what shall we buy mother as a souvenir? A marzipan heart, of course. And father? A gingerbread man.

August 8
THE SEVEN RAVENS

Once upon a time there was a queen who came from a poor and very large family. With her seven brothers there were, altogether, eight children in their cottage. The king chose her as his wife because she was beautiful, kind and hard-working.

When some time had passed, a son was born to the happy king and queen, but a witch who hated the king carried the baby off. When the queen's seven brothers went looking for it she changed them into seven ravens. But worse, the witch convinced the king that the queen herself had done away with the infant.

The queen was about to be burned at the stake for her deed. In fact she was already tied to the stake when her seven raven brothers appeared, carrying the child in a sling. The king set his queen free at once, and had the witch burned in her place.

124

August 9
THE TWO STUBBORN GOATS

Two goats were grazing alongside a mountain stream, a white one on one bank, a black one on the other. By and by, they both came to the footbridge, and each of them decided to cross to the other side. They met in the middle of the bridge, and soon realized that they could not get past each other, since the bridge was too narrow.

'Out of my way!' said the white goat.

'Out of my way!' said the black goat.

Then they pushed each other, and butted each other, until they both fell in the water. The next time they wanted to cross over to graze on the other side, they didn't bother to use the bridge; they both waded through the stream instead.

August 10
THE LITTLE GIRL WHO LIKED PEAS

A little girl who loved sweet green peas more than anything decided to build herself a little doll's cottage in the garden from ripe pea pods. The pods in the bed ripened quickly, but one day the girl went to the pea bed and saw that all of them had been husked and podded. The little girl said to herself that she must find out who had done this to her peas.

She lay down by the pea bed, and resolved not to blink an eyelid, and to keep careful watch. But before long her

eyes grew heavy, and she dropped off to sleep. When she woke up, there were even more empty pods than there had been before. So the little girl set off to follow the trail of pods to see where it led to. It took her straight into the yard to where the duck and the goose had their pens!

August **11**

THE DUCK AND THE GOOSE

The little girl who liked peas knocked on the duck's door and pointed to the empty pea pods lying outside.

'The wind must have blown them there,' said the duck.

The little girl knocked on the goose's door.

'What do you mean?' said the goose, indignantly. 'I keep a sharp eye on all my goslings, and never let them into the garden.'

Both the birds told her that peas were not to the liking of ducks and geese at all, anyway, and that that sort of thing was more in the line of those uncouth hens. The little girl decided the best thing to do was to pick all the peas that were left, and she and her mother gathered all the rest of the peas the very same day.

August **12**

JIMMY AT THE MILL

Every year, in the summer holidays, Jimmy would go to visit his grandfather at the mill. Grandfather knew no end of stories and fairy tales, and many of them were all about the green dwarf who lived in the stream.

'Once a bear-keeper and his bear spent the night here,' grandfather told him. 'They slept in the grinding-room where the green dwarf used to fry himself fish every night. The clanging of the frying-pan must have woken the bear up. He smelled the fish cooking, got up, and started to take the fish out of the pan. The green dwarf rapped him on the knuckles with a wooden spoon. The bear scratched him with his claws and drove him out of the mill. Since then he has never shown his face here again, and has lived in the stream ever since.'

August 13

GRANDFATHER'S MESSAGE

Jimmy went swimming in the fishpond every day. He had learnt to swim long ago, but when he saw the ducks diving, he was so envious of them, that he took a fancy to diving himself. He pestered his parents so much, that in the end they gave in and bought him some diving goggles and a pair of flippers.

Now Jimmy really had a fine time! He dived, and dived, and each time he went down he expected to meet the green dwarf down there in the underwater realm. Didn't his grandfather keep reminding him to tell the fellow that there had been no bear in the grinding-room for ages now?

But maybe Jimmy couldn't see very well under the water, or maybe the green dwarf had moved off somewhere else. Anyway, he hasn't been back to the mill since.

so fast that it was too big for the bath-tub.

The green dwarf fried one portion after another, and invited everyone in the mill to join in the feast.

'We all had a great time when the dwarf was here,' said grandfather. 'A pity he doesn't come any more.'

That night Jimmy dreamed he brought home a fish that grew, and grew, until the water from the bath flooded the whole house. He was relieved when he woke up and found he'd been dreaming.

August 15

THE PEASANT-WOMAN WHO DANCED WITH THE DEVILS

There was once a farmer who had a very pretty and pleasant wife. There was just one thing about her that worried him. Every night she locked herself in the

August 14

THE FISH THAT GREW BEFORE YOUR VERY EYES

One of grandfather's stories was about a fish that grew before your very eyes. He said that one day the green dwarf brought such a fish to the mill, and put it in the bath. Before he had even heated up the fat in the pan, the fish had grown

back room. Every morning she was sleepy and pale, and her shoes were worn away with dancing.

The farmer longed to find out what was going on. So he called his shepherd and told him to hide behind the door of the back room that night, and to watch what went on there.

Before midnight had finished striking, a black carriage pulled up outside the farmhouse. The peasant-woman climbed in, and before the carriage drove off the shepherd managed to jump up on the footboard at the back. On and on they drove, and before you wake up again, they will be back.

August **16**

HOW THE SHEPHERD SET THE PEASANT-WOMAN FREE

Through the rear window of the carriage the shepherd could see the farmer's wife and three devils. The road passed through a rosemary wood, and the shepherd plucked a sprig. He did the same when they passed through a rose wood and a lily wood. At last they arrived at a black castle, where the peasant-woman danced all night with the devils.

The next morning the shepherd told the farmer the whole story, and gave him the sprigs he had picked on the way. The farmer stroked his wife with the three sprigs, and, in tears, she told him all. She had once refused to dance with a certain farm-lad. 'I should rather dance with devils than with you,' she had said, and since then the devils had never left her in peace. Only the sprigs plucked by the shepherd set her free.

August **17**

THE FROG AND THE WITCH

There was once a frog in the fishpond who wanted to be as big as a bull and as fat as a heifer.

She went to ask the witch if this was possible, and the witch told her, 'Just puff yourself up, and you will be big and fat too.'

The frog blew herself up until she burst.

'You made a mistake that time,' said the witch's husband, and he sprinkled the frog with the water of life. When the frog had come back to life again, he told her, 'You must go and graze in the meadow like the bull and the heifer, and you will grow big and fat.'

The frog tried it. She bit off a few green blades, but she just moved them back and forth in her mouth until she almost choked. Somehow she just couldn't bring herself to swallow the grass. However could the bull and the heifer eat something as nasty as grass? 'I'd rather stay the size I am,' thought the frog. And she plopped back into the water.

SPECIAL GLOVES FOR JENNY

Poor Jenny! All her friends were on holiday and she had caught measles. She was very bored after the second week, but one day her favourite aunt came to visit her.

'I bought you a pair of gloves,' said her aunt, with a twinkle in her eye. 'Gloves,' thought Jenny. 'What an odd present.' But she opened the bag and what do you think was inside? Not a pair of gloves, but a pair of glove puppets.

'Thank you,' she cried, hugging her aunt and trying to put the puppets on at the same time.

After that, she wasn't bored at all and almost enjoyed being ill with her glove puppets to play with.

August **19**

THE CLOWN AND HIS DOG

All the children were waiting happily for the clown to begin his act. The curtains opened, and there he was. With him was his little dog. 'Tell me, little dog,' said the clown. 'What's the difference between an elephant and a post box?' 'I don't know,' barked the dog. 'Well, I'm never going to send you to post a letter, that's for sure,' said the clown.

The dog didn't seem to like that joke,

or the next one, or the one after and began to bark so loudly that the children could not hear what the clown said.

So the children began to shout at the dog to go away and leave the clown in peace. 'You'll be sorry,' barked the dog as it trotted off.

A few minutes later the curtains suddenly came down. Who do you think had pulled the string? — that's right, the dog.

'I didn't know you could do that,' said the clown. 'Well, now you do,' woofed the dog. 'You can teach old dogs new tricks, you know.'

August **20**

THE ROUNDABOUTS

Johnny climbed up on the elephant, little Lizzie onto the duck, and Freddy, as he did at every village fair, sat in the saddle of his bay mare. The music began to play 'Over the Hills and Far Away'. Freddy and his bay mare gave a leap, and went into a gallop.

'Gee up, bay mare, let's ride past Johnny on his elephant and Lizzie on her duck!' Freddy called.

But no matter how fast the bay mare went, the elephant and the duck stayed as far ahead as ever. When the roundabout had stopped Johnny stayed on, but the others said that he was wasting his time — the bay mare would never catch up. I suppose they were right.

August 21

THE CUNNING VAGABOND

One day, during the fair, a cunning robber came into the village. He knew very well that he would find all the food he wanted in any house, as everyone would be at the fair.

He stole unnoticed into the first farmhouse and took a roast goose straight from the oven. From the next house he took a hare, from the third a stuffed pheasant. But this time they caught him, and took him off to the village magistrate.

'Now then, scoundrel, tell me everything you have done,' said the magistrate. 'I forced a goose out of an oven,' said the cunning fellow. 'How good of you! What else?' asked the magistrate. 'And a hare; I made it leave some potatoes.' 'We are lucky you came to our village,' said the magistrate. 'If you hadn't driven off the goose and the hare, these poor people would have gone hungry.'

The scoundrel was given a reward and was told to stay in the village as long as he wanted — but he left that very day!

August 22

GRANDMA AND GRANDDAD HAVE A DANCE

When Freddy came running into Grandma and Granddad's house to ask for some money for the roundabout, they were prancing about gaily. They were dancing a clockwise country reel, al-

though the parlour was scarcely big enough. The dog, afraid of getting his tail trampled on, had jumped on a chair in the corner for safety.

'Oh, how my head is spinning,' said Granny, quite out of breath. 'Catch me, Freddy, or I shall fall down.'

'Don't worry, Granny, I'll unwind you,' said Freddy, and he danced an anti-clockwise reel with her. When he had finished, Granny wasn't dizzy any more and she gave him money for the roundabout.

August 23

GRANDMA, THE LITTLE PRINCESS AND THE DRAGONS

The little princess sat, enraptured, as her grandmother told her a fairy tale about dragons before she went to sleep. So real did she make the fire-breathing monsters seem that the princess fell asleep and dreamed about them.

In her dream she saw two dragons, with ever-so-long tongues hanging out of their mouths. It was a wonder they didn't start licking her face.

'Don't you know how rude it is to put out your tongues?' the princess shouted at them. 'It is clear that you have not been brought up properly.' And, do you know what? The dragons put away their tongues, and were as good as a pair of well-behaved dogs.

August 24

THE MOUSE THAT ATE THE GOLD

A Persian merchant once had to go on a business trip. He gave his neighbour, the carter, a hundredweight of gold to look after for him. On his return he wanted the gold back again.

'Gold?' said the carter. 'I am sorry to say the mice have eaten all the gold.'

That night the merchant took the carter's horses from his stable. In the morning the carter came lamenting to the merchant, asking how he was to make a living without his horses.

'I saw some owls carry your horses off in the night,' the merchant told him.

'I don't believe it,' said the carter. 'How could owls carry off a horse?'

'In a land where mice eat gold, owls may carry off horses!' replied the merchant.

The carter was ashamed of himself. He gave the merchant back his gold, and his horses were returned to him.

August 25

THE SHEPHERD AND THE PRINCESS

Princess Flaxenhair had fallen in love

with a shepherd boy but the king would not let her marry him. He decided to hold a great tournament to decide who should marry his daughter. Noble lords and princes from the four corners of the earth were to compete for the hand of the princess. Whoever rode up to her first, unfastened the silk scarf from her throat, and took the ring from her finger would win her for his wife.

The horses galloped off and an unknown rider reached the princess first. He took off her scarf and slipped the ring from her finger. He then raised his vizor. The princess cried out in delight, for it was her shepherd-boy and the king had to let her marry him after all.

DACSH THE DOG AND HIS MISTRESS

When Dacsh the dog was a little puppy, nothing annoyed him more than the fact that he trod on his front paws with his back ones while he was walking.

'Why did my hind legs grow so near my forelegs?' he grumbled, and he asked his mistress what he was to do.

'You must do your exercises, Dacsh,' she told him. 'Do your exercises and stretch yourself out.'

From then on Dacsh did his exercises every day. And look at him now! His

134

back seems to have grown a little bit too long if anything — but it suits him that way.

Some time after that, Dacsh's mistress put on a little weight, and it was her turn to ask him what she should do. He advised her to do a lot of walking, and every day he takes her for a long, long walk.

August 27

EVEN FOXES GET CAUGHT OUT SOMETIMES

A greedy young fox caught a swan in the farmyard and ran off to the woods with him. On the way the swan said to him, 'You are not a bit like your father. The first thing he always did was to put the swan down on a tree stump and give thanks for successful hunting.'

'What makes you think I wasn't going to?' asked the fox haughtily. He put the swan down on a tree stump and began to give thanks. In a trice the swan flapped his wings and flew *trrh* — into the nearest tree, well out of the fox's way.

August 28

JUDE AND THE RAVENS

One day young Jude decided he must find the wolf which had been carrying off the shepherd's sheep during the night.

He jumped on his horse and rode off. In the woods nearby he came across a raven's nest. 'The ravens may know something about the wolf,' he thought; 'but how am I to get them to tell me?'

As Jude wondered how to make friends with the ravens, he remembered the nuts in his pocket. He had picked them on the way. He gave one to each of the ravens, then asked them if they knew where the wolf lived.

'Klark, klark,' said the ravens. 'Follow us, we'll take you there.'

August 29

JUDE RESCUES THE LAMBS

On the way the ravens shelled the nuts, and by following the trail of shells, Jude came to the wolf's lair deep in the forest.

He banged on the door and called out, 'I've come for the lambs that you stole.'

'What lambs?' shouted the wolf, not opening the door. 'I know nothing about lambs.'

136

But just then some of the lambs having heard Jude's knocking began to bleat loudly and the wolf had to let them out.

'Don't do that again,' said Jude, 'or else . . .'

'Or else what?' asked the wolf.

'Or else we'll peck your eyes out,' croaked the ravens.

The wolf never did steal a single lamb from that day on.

August 30

HOW THE COWBOY HERDED BISON

There was once a cowboy who didn't know anything about anything except how to look after cows and bulls, so he couldn't find a job for a long time. As he wandered from ranch to ranch looking for work, he spotted in the middle of the prairie a cowboy hat in a tree. He drew nearer and saw that there was another cowboy sitting in the tree.

'Hi there,' he called up. 'What are you doing up there, birdnesting?'

The cowboy in the tree put his finger

to his lips and whispered, 'Not so loud! I'm herding bison, and if I were you, I should get up the tree too as quick as you can—they've already got wind of you.'

Quick as a flash the cowboy was up the tree—I wonder if he's still there.

August 31

CHESTNUT THE HARE

Once upon a time there was a row of chestnut trees where a hare and his wife lived. They were happy there, but the one thing which upset them was that they had no children.

One day a chestnut fell down in front of their cottage. It was still inside its green cover, with a piece of twig attached to it. The hare's wife nursed it in her arms, and all of a sudden a baby hare jumped out of it.

Because he had come out of a chestnut and was chestnut-coloured, they called him Chestnut.

Although Chestnut was born when autumn was almost here, he was soon as large as the March hares. When he grew up, he set out into the world. And where did he get to? We'll see tomorrow.

CHESTNUT THE HARE AND THE CABBAGE

Chestnut the hare liked the look of a nearby cabbage field. Maybe it was because he had come out of a green chestnut skin, and the green cabbages reminded him of it. Anyway, Chestnut wanted to make himself a parlour in one of the cabbages.

But the moment he began, the cabbage went *snap!* and caught hold of the little hare. He could have stayed there all winter, but luckily a farmer came along one day to cut the cabbages. The cabbage let Chestnut go, and he quickly ran back to his mother and father and the safety of the chestnut alley.

HOW TOMMY BECAME A WINDOW DRESSER

Five-year-old Tommy got a big box of modelling clay for his birthday, as well as a cake and five candles.

The first thing he wanted to model was Albert the dog.

'Are you going to do me sitting down, or running about?' asked Albert.

'Oh no!' said Millie the cat, who was just a little jealous. 'He is sure to model you standing on your tail.'

'It's just like a real dog,' Daddy told Tommy that evening. The next morning he borrowed Tommy's model dog and put it in the window of his ironmonger's shop in the town square. He put a collar with a lead around its neck. The next day he had sold out of dog collars, so when he got a delivery of milk bowls, he asked Tommy to make a model of Millie the cat.

September 3

THE GAMEKEEPER

It was the hunting season and the game-keeper was very busy. Every day he was rushing hither and thither, from morning to night, not even going home for lunch. His wife began to complain that she never saw him. 'I'm much too busy,' he would say to her when she complained every night when he got home. He was so tired that he went straight to bed as soon as he had had his supper.

'I'm going to call you Jack from now on,' said his wife one morning.

'But my name's Hans,' said the game-keeper.

'Well,' his wife replied, 'all work and no play makes Jack a dull fellow and that's just what you've become.'

After that Hans did not work *quite* so hard.

September 4

KITE-FLYING

The wind began to blow, to puff, to bluster off the stubble. From the banks and hillsides the kites began to fly: big ones, little ones, all shapes and sizes.

'Don't forget, children,' said mother, when she had helped the boys and girls to make their kites, 'that the weights are as important as the sticks and paper.

You'd better wait for Daddy to come home, he knows more about it than I do.'

When Daddy came home from work, the children gathered round and, all at the same time, pleaded with him to put the weights on their kites, because they were most important. 'Of course I will,' he told them. 'But do you know what is most important of all when you're flying kites?'

'No!' cried the children.

'Why, the wind, of course,' said their father.

September **5**

TOMMY, THE SQUIRREL AND THE NUTCRACKERS

Just as the hazel-nuts were beginning to ripen, Sammy the squirrel turned up in the summer house. Sammy lived in the park next door to Tommy's house.

'My nutcrackers are broken, Tommy,' he said. 'Have a word with your father at the ironmonger's, will you? What

would I do without my nutcrackers?'

When Tommy and the squirrel arrived at the shop, Tommy's father offered to change the nutcrackers if Sammy would agree to sit in the shopwindow.

'You know very well that Sammy the squirrel doesn't even like people staring at him in the park,' said Tommy.

'That's true,' said Daddy. 'All right, then, let him model for you in the summer-house.'

When Sammy nodded his agreement, Tommy's father gave him a brand new pair of nutcrackers.

September **6**

WHEN THE WIND WON'T BLOW

Katie was free this afternoon, and she was looking forward to flying her kite till evening. But, just to be awkward, there was not a breath of wind to stir the leaves. The sun shone as in mid-summer, and there was not even the tiniest breeze.

'There's no need to pull such a face,' the robin comforted her. 'Tomorrow is another day.'

'And will the wind blow tomorrow at last?' asked Katie.

'You never can tell with the wind,' chirped the robin. 'But I've got a feeling it will blow tomorrow.'

September 7

A KITE GETS CAUGHT IN THE APPLE-TREE

The next day, as the robin had said, the wind did blow — and how! Katie's kite shot up like an arrow. The wind took it higher and higher, till it was a wonder Katie didn't get dizzy, so high up and far away it seemed.

When Katie had let out all her string, the wind snatched it from her hands and for a while jerked it to and fro. In the end it flung the kite into an apple-tree.

Just as the robin had comforted her yesterday, so the blue-tit helped her today.

'I'll get it for you, Katie,' she twittered, and she carefully brought down the kite to her.

September 8

TOMMY MODELS A SQUIRREL

While he was modelling the squirrel, Tommy had the greatest trouble making the fur look real. But in the end he got it right.

'Come and have a look at yourself, Sammy,' he said. 'What do you think?'

'That's me?' The squirrel blushed with delight. And he kept saying how nice it was of Tommy to make such a lovely model of him.

Tommy fastened the broken nutcrackers to the model squirrel's paws.

'Now it's all ready, Sammy,' he said.

'Tomorrow morning we'll go and see how you look in the window of Daddy's shop.'

September 9

THE KITE-FLYING CONTEST

The boys and girls held a kite-flying competition, to see whose kite could fly furthest and highest.

Little Katie entered her kite. After the accident with the apple-tree, she kept looking round for the robin and the blue-tit, so that they could perhaps help her out of trouble again if necessary.

'The gold one with green glasses on wins; the gold one is the winner!' the children shouted. And who do you think

was on the other end of the string? Why, little Katie, all smiles.

September 10

FLIPPITY THE IMP

As the autumn drew on, Tommy got some new things to model with in the summer-house. Now he had not only modelling clay, but also chestnuts, acorns, oak-apples and chestnut and maple leaves.

He used them to make an imp with one bird's leg and one human one. He christened him Flippity. That evening he took the imp to show his father, and he couldn't wait to see what he thought of it.

'I'm afraid your Flippity is not quite

right for an ironmonger's window,' his father said, 'but if we sold books of fairy tales, all the children might stop to look at him, and I'm sure they would all like him!'

September 11

THE SQUIRREL MOVES HOUSE

Tommy and the squirrel became firm friends. Tommy persuaded him to stay in the garden.

So they set off for the park at once to bring the squirrel's possessions.

But no one would believe the number of boxes, jars, pots, cups and strange containers a squirrel's house has in it. And every one of them had a label on it to say what it contained. One said 'hazel-nuts in sugar'. Another said 'salted hazel-nuts'. Another said 'walnut preserve'. And 'beech-nuts', 'oak-

apples', 'blackberries', 'strawberries', 'elderberries', 'lime-flowers', 'rose-hips', and so on, and so on.

It was no easy matter to collect it all together and take it safely to the summer-house. The squirrel then carried it all up into the oak tree himself, and he lives there in a cosy little hollow to this day.

September 12

THE COWHERD

All the cows looked horrified as they saw that the grass and clover in the fields had been cut down. 'Where is it?' they asked the cowherd. 'In the barn,' said the cowherd. 'You will eat it in the winter when there is nothing else.' 'But what are we to eat now?' they moaned. 'Just you wait until tomorrow,' said the cowherd.

That night it rained and the next morning the grass and clover were beginning to grow again. The cowherd

gave the cows some of the hay that had been harvested and the same thing happened the day after and the day after. But soon the fields were covered with sweet new grass and the cows munched happily.

a good idea who was calling. It wasn't hard to guess: why, we could guess ourselves — we know which little girl likes peas best, don't we?

Do you remember the story we read in August? Of course you do.

September 13

WILL GORDON SOW PEAS?

Gordon had just finished ploughing the stubble, and was hitching the oxen to the harrow to get ready to sow winter wheat. Just then a voice called from somewhere, 'Don't sow wheat, Gordon, sow peas!'

The two oxen turned towards the river and stared in disbelief, for there was not a soul in sight, not even a little bird. But Gordon just smiled. He had

---

September 14

NUTCRACKERS, COLLARS, CHAINS FOR SALE!

Tommy set off one day with Albert the dog, Millie the cat and Sammy the squirrel for his father's ironmonger's shop. Long before they got there they saw a queue of people waiting to buy nutcrackers, and another queue of dog owners who wanted to buy collars and chains.

'Look, it's him,' cried one of the nutcracker queue. 'The one who's in the window!'

'It's him, it's him!' cried the dog owners, pointing to Albert.

Tommy's father didn't have time to speak to him, or to the dog, or the cat, or the squirrel. He just managed to tell Tommy that the milk bowls had just arrived, and that he had better get the model of Millie the cat finished quickly.

September 15

WHERE THE MUSHROOMS GROW

One day, after school, a little girl called Betty set off into the woods to look for mushrooms. She met a squirrel.

'Squirrel,' she asked, 'you know everything about the woods; tell me where the mushrooms grow.'

'Dear me,' said the squirrel, 'if you were to ask me where the hazel-nuts grow, then I could tell you. But I don't know anything about mushrooms, my dear. Wait a minute, though, why don't you ask the slug? He knows every toadstool and mushroom in the forest.'

They went to ask the slug. He just smiled craftily and said, 'Mushrooms grow in that part of the forest where the very first ray of the sun falls every morning. That's where you must look!'

'And where does the sun's first ray fall?' asked Betty.

'You'll only find that out,' the cunning

slug said, 'if you go mushrooming before sunrise, not in the afternoon after school.'

September **16**

THE MODELLING OF MILLIE THE CAT

Sammy the squirrel was a great help to Tommy when he was making a model of Millie the cat. He even came up with his very own ideas. He suggested using nut shells for the pussy's ears. Then he proposed that they should make the nose out of a beech-nut.

They used a couple of pieces of mica (which is sometimes called cat-silver) for the eyes. (But that was Albert's idea.) Then it took them a long time to decide what to make the claws out of. In the end they used the thorns from the dry branch of a wild rose-bush.

And the cat was splendid, just like the real Millie. You would have thought it would have come to life, so real did it look. Tommy's father *was* pleased.

September **17**

WHO'S BEEN AT THE CREAM?

It seemed to Mummy that the cream jug was getting emptier day by day.

'We shall have to keep a sharp eye on the cream jug, Katie. I can't help thinking someone has been taking our cream.'

'Whoever would do that?' replied Katie, blushing hotly.

'I can't think who it might be,' said Mummy. 'Could it be the cat? Or some-

one else with a sweet tooth? Where is the cat? Have you seen her?'

Then Katie grew even redder and owned up.

'I'm the one with the sweet tooth, Mummy, not the cat,' she said. And instead of being cross, her mother told her what a good girl she was for owning up.

September **18**

THE FARMER AND THE CABBAGES

Someone had been at the farmer's cabbages again. Whoever it was, had peeled some of the leaves from the heads, and disappeared without trace.

At first the farmer had suspected the hares and the roe deer. But, one morning, he found a basket in the field, forgotten or dropped by someone who had left in a hurry. It was filled to the brim with cabbage leaves. So, he said to himself, it was not the animals who were to blame, but someone from the village.

He scratched his head for a long time, trying to think who it might be. He knew the basket well enough. He had seen it many times filled with grass, mushrooms or apples.

So he decided to set out for the village at once.

September 19

THE FARMHAND HAS A VISITOR

A farmhand was sitting in the tavern in

front of a tankard of ale. The farmer set a basket of cabbage leaves down on the table and asked the farmhand if he knew whose it was.

'It be our Nancy's,' replied the farmhand.

'Then I have her, the thief. She's been stealing cabbages from my field,' roared the farmer.

'Come now, Mr Giles, what do you mean stealing?' asked the farmhand. 'Nancy dug your cabbages all year round. She has only taken her due.'

'That's as may be,' the farmer said. 'But it is my field.'

Just then Nancy appeared with a delicious bowl of cabbage soup for the farmer. It was so good he forgot his

anger and told Nancy to take as many cabbages as she wanted whenever she liked, from then on.

September 20

THE RAVEN, THE FOX AND THE CHEESE

A raven once sat in a tree with some cheese in his beak. The smell of the cheese brought the fox out of his den.

The fox came up to the tree and began to flatter the raven. 'How well your black coat suits you, good raven,' began the foxy flatterer. 'I should very much like to hear the sound of your voice, for I am sure it is finer than that of the king himself.'

And, of course, the minute the raven

148

opened his beak to agree with the fox, the cheese fell straight into the waiting fox's open jaws!

The king had to admit the truth of these words, so he kept his horse and left the fisherman his net.

September **21**

THE KING AND THE FISHERMAN

One day, while out hunting, a king came to the banks of a lake, where an old fisherman and his son were making a fishing net.

'You have a fine net, fisherman,' said the king. 'I shall buy it from you.'

'I do not make nets for sale, sire,' said the fisherman. 'But you are my king, and I shall give you this net, if you will give me your horse.'

'Why do you want a horse in return for a fishing net?' asked the king, in surprise.

'Just as you need your horse for your hunting, so I need a net for my fishing,' replied the fisherman.

September **22**

THE BOY AND THE BIRD

One afternoon some children were playing close to the zoo. It was already starting to get dark, when one little boy went wandering off from the rest. He was getting very tired when he came to what he thought was a hill. He climbed up it, and found a warm and comfortable spot where he lay down to rest. In a while he fell fast asleep.

When he woke up, he found the whole mountain was moving. When he took a closer look, he saw that he had gone to sleep on the back of some huge bird.

'I want to go home!' he shouted, banging on the bird's back.

'I can't take you as far as that,' the

bird replied, 'but try to hold tight.'

What a ride that was! In a little while they were at the ZOO gates. From there it wasn't far to go home, and the little boy spent the whole evening telling everyone about the ride he had on a huge bird.

September 23

PRINCESS GOLDIE

Princess Goldie liked to sit beside the garden fountain. One day, as she was sitting there weaving herself a garland of flowers, a green frog jumped up on the rim of the fountain.

'Wherever did you come from, little frog?' she asked.

'Where there's water, you'll always find me,' said the frog.

'And why have you come?'

'If you don't think I'm too ugly, then stroke me,' the frog told her.

'I don't think you are ugly at all,' said the princess and stroked him gently.

In an instant a handsome young man was standing before her.

September 24

PRINCESS GOLDIE AND THE FROG PRINCE

When the young man thanked Princess Goldie for releasing him, she retorted indignantly that she hadn't released anyone, only stroked a little green frog. 'But, Princess,' said the young man. 'That was me, I was under a spell.'

'Then you had better get back under it this minute!' the princess told him.

'If you promise to stroke me again,' the young man replied.

When the princess agreed, the young

little friends where to hide when the hunters came into the woods and shots began to ring out among the trees. 'Why don't you dampen their powder?' asked the hare. 'Because I'm a gamekeeper.' 'Well, you want to keep the game, don't you?' And the gamekeeper had to agree.

September 26

THE STAG AND THE DUKE

One day the duke, himself, came into the forest to hunt. He was the best shot in the area and all the animals were terrified of him.

But the wise old stag came up with the ideal solution.

'Camouflage,' he said to the animals. 'We'll all camouflage ourselves and the duke will not be able to see us.'

man changed back into a frog. But now the frog said, 'When you stroke me, promise to marry me.'

Princess Goldie was happy to promise, and before long a great wedding was held at the palace.

September 25

WILL THE HUNTER'S POWDER GET WET?

The autumn hunting and shooting season was drawing near.

One gamekeeper, who had a hare by his side instead of a hunting dog, and carried a blackbird about on his hat, would have liked to hide all the pheasants, hares and deer in his hunting lodge until it was all over, if he could, for he was very kind-hearted.

But since they wouldn't all have fitted inside, he roamed anxiously about the forest, and wherever he went he told his

So they cut branches and leaves off the trees and stuck them to each other so that they blended into the forest perfectly and no one could see them.

When the duke arrived he looked and looked, but no matter where he went there was no sign of any animal to hunt. After a few hours he was so disgusted he went home and didn't bother the animals in the forest again for the rest of the hunting season.

September **27**

THE FARMER, THE HORSE AND THE FOX

One day, a farmer drove his old horse off the farm. 'You're good for nothing now!' he told the poor creature. 'Don't you come back again unless you drag a lion with you, to prove that you still have some strength left!'

The horse went into the forest to hide from the rain and the sun. He met a fox and he told him how the farmer had treated him. He asked where he was to find the strength necessary to overcome a lion.

'I'll help you,' the fox told him. 'Lie here in the grass and pretend to be dead.' And off he ran.

'I'll take a nap till he gets back,' thought the horse, and he closed his eyes and slept, and slept.

September 28

HOW THE FOX HELPED THE HORSE

In a nearby village there happened to be a circus, with lots of animals — elephants, lions and bears.

The fox came running up to the lions, and said to one of them, 'There is a dead horse in the forest; come with me, and you shall have a good breakfast.'

The lion, of course, agreed, and when they got to the horse, the fox said, 'This is not too pleasant a spot for a meal. I'll tell you what — I'll tie the horse to your tail, and you can drag him off home and eat him in comfort.'

The lion agreed, and waited patiently while the cunning fox tied all his paws together with the horse's tail.

When he had finished, the fox slapped the horse's flank and said, 'Pull, pull!'

The horse dragged the lion off to the farmer, who told him, 'You shall stay with me, old fellow, and shall want for nothing for the rest of your life.'

The horse was so grateful to the fox that whenever the fox needed shelter, he hid him safely in his stable.

September 29

THE BITTERN AND THE HOOPOE

The sheep had eaten all the grass on the mountain slopes during spring and summer, so the shepherd began looking for new pastures for the autumn.

Young Jude offered to ride into the woods on his horse, to ask his friends the birds where there was good pasture. All the birds he asked knew the countryside very well from their wanderings through the forests, and tried to help him.

'Hoop, hoop, hoop,' the hoopoe told him. 'Send them higher up!'

'Boom, boom,' said the bittern. 'Send them lower down!'

'A great help you are!' said Jude. He thanked the birds, and rode on.

September 30

HOW THE HORSE FOUND NEW PASTURES

Jude was still pondering over the strange advice the hoopoe and the bittern had given him, when his horse pricked up his ears and came to a halt. Then the horse galloped off through the trees of his own accord. Before they had gone far, a green meadow appeared in the distance. 'But will it be big enough for the

whole flock?' thought Jude to himself. And it certainly was. It was almost as big as the spring and summer pastures put together.

'We've found our autumn pastures!' Jude called out with glee, sinking his fingers deep in the horse's mane. 'You must have understood the hoopoe and the bittern better than I did.'

'Not surprising really,' said the horse. 'Animals understand each other much better than humans do.'

October 1

THE ODD PLANT

An old man was quite lost in a forest. The more he tried to find his way home, the more lost he became. After several hours he stopped by a very odd-looking plant.

Suddenly the wind whispered to him, 'If you ask the plant the way to go home it will tell you. But be careful, for only one leaf tells the truth.'

The old man did as the wind had told him. One leaf pointed upwards and the man knew that it was telling a lie. Another pointed downwards, so the old man knew that it, too, was not telling the truth. But one leaf pointed straight ahead, so the old man followed it and soon arrived safely home.

October 2

THE PRINCESS WITH THE LONG NOSE

One day a young prince came and asked a proud princess to marry him. But she cruelly refused.

As he made his way home he passed an old beggar woman who asked him for a few pennies, which he gave her.

She thanked him kindly and said, 'You have come from the proud princess, haven't you? I can make her marry you.'

She gave the prince two bunches of cherries. 'Give her the black ones. The princess loves cherries and will gladly take them. But when she eats them her nose will grow and grow. You must tell her that only if she promises to marry you will her nose become normal again. When she makes the promise, give her the red ones and her nose will shrink.'

Everything happened as the old lady said it would and the princess married the prince whom she came to love deeply.

October 3

THE HUNTER AND THE RABBIT

A hunter went into the woods one day to try to shoot some fine, plump rabbits for his wife to cook for supper. As he walked into the woods he sang to himself:

'It's good to eat rice, but rabbit's so nice.'

A badger heard the hunter sing and was very sad, for the rabbits in the woods were his friends. He ran to tell a little boy who came to play in the woods every day.

'You must hide,' the boy told the rabbits.

'It is too late,' said the badger.

They all looked round and saw that the hunter was approaching. Just then there was a tremendous thud and an enormous chestnut fell to the ground. As it fell it cracked open and it was so big that a rabbit could easily hide in it.

'If only there were more,' said the boy, 'you could all hide.'

No sooner had he spoken than his pony began to shake the tree with all his might and nut after nut fell to the ground. All the rabbits scampered into a nutshell and hid there safely until the hunter had passed. How puzzled he was when he did not see a single rabbit all day.

October **4**

THE BANANA SKIN

'Did I ever tell you about the time I was in the Arctic?' asked Uncle Johnny.

The children did not like him very much. No matter what anyone had done, Uncle Johnny had always done it better.

'Everyone had fallen in the snow and broken their ankles,' Uncle Johnny went

on. 'I walked through the snow for mile after mile to get help. No one else could have done it. They wanted to give me a hero's welcome for what I had done, but I was much too modest for that, much too modest.'

Just then Uncle Johnny slipped on a banana skin. 'Help,' he cried. 'I've broken my ankle.'

The children tried hard not to giggle, but it was very difficult.

October 5

THE PRINCESS AND THE PEA

There was once a prince who was determined to marry a *real* princess, but he could not find one he liked. One evening a terrible storm broke and there was a knocking at the castle door. When the queen opened it she found a girl standing there. She claimed to be a *real* princess.

'We'll soon see about that,' thought the queen and showed the girl up to a bedchamber. While the princess was drying herself the queen took twenty mattresses and laid them on top of a pea.

The next morning the queen asked the princess how she had slept.

'Miserably,' cried the girl. 'I lay on something so hard that I hardly slept.'

So the royal family knew that she was a *real* princess, for only a *real* princess could have felt a pea through so many mattresses.

October 6

THE BRAVE KNIGHT

Brave Sir Arthur rode out one day from his fine castle in search of adventure. But it was very quiet that day.

Disheartened, the brave knight decided to return home. But suddenly he heard a girl scream, 'HELP!'

The voice was coming from an open window. Sir Arthur jumped onto his horse's back and drew his shining sword. He rode up to the window.

When he looked into the room he was disappointed to find a charming girl standing on a stool, holding her skirts around her. She was frightened of a mouse. Sir Arthur chased the mouse

away and the damsel was just as grateful as if it had been a dragon he had saved her from.

October **7**

THE HAUNTED WISHING WELL

A man once entered a completely deserted town. When he passed the well he saw some ghosts around it. 'Who are you and what do you want?' asked one of the ghosts.

'I am looking for work,' said the man.

'There is no work here,' said another ghost. 'We own this town. When we came here no one would give us what we wanted, so we put all the townsfolk to

sleep until we could find someone to help us.'

'What is it that you are looking for?' asked the man.

'A place to sleep forever. Because we were wicked when we lived we must roam the world until someone gives us his blessing.'

The man drew some water from the well and blessed the ghosts with it. As soon as he had done so they disappeared and the people awoke from their enchanted sleep and rewarded the man for freeing them.

October 8

SILLY SOPHY

Sophy's mother said, 'Get up,
I want to take you out with Pup;
And I have a little plan
To go and visit with your Gran.'

But Sophy shook her little head
And said she'd rather stay in bed.

Her mother went off, very angry
And let poor Sophy stay there —

       hungry.

October 9

THE GENTLE SHEPHERD

One day a shepherd lost one of his sheep. He searched all that day and the next and the next but there was no sign of it.

'You have plenty of other sheep,' said a neighbour. 'Stop looking.'

But the shepherd carried on looking, and a few days later when he was sitting on top of a cliff he heard his sheep bleating down below. He looked over the

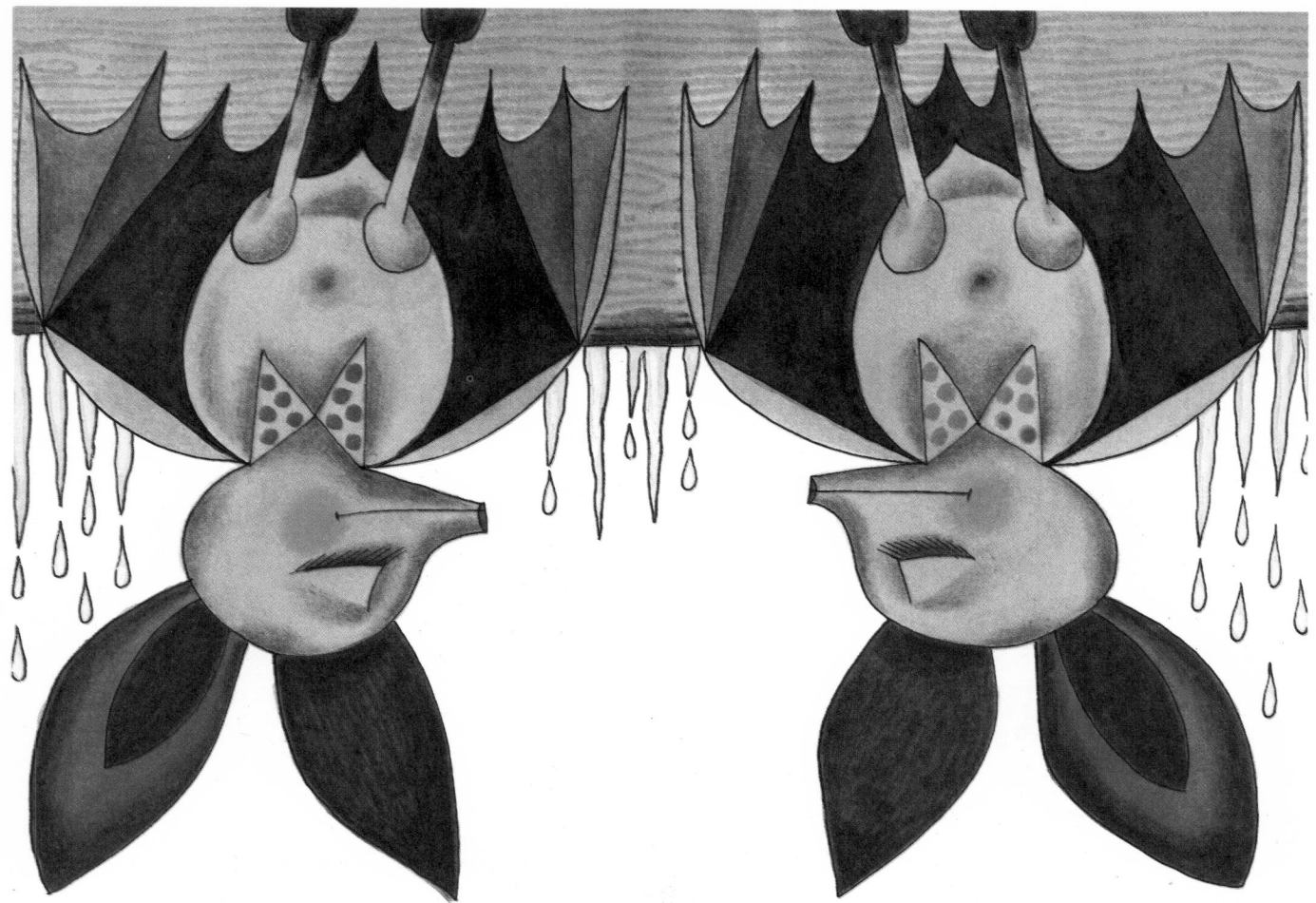

edge and saw it, stranded on a ledge. He carefully climbed down and helped the sheep back to safety.

'I didn't think he would care about one sheep,' the relieved animal whispered to the shepherd's dog. 'After all he has plenty more.'

'That doesn't matter to him,' said the dog. 'He loves all his sheep and even if he had a million of them he would still treat each one as if it was the most important.'

October 10

BIG EARS

Everyone laughed at the little orphan and called him Big Ears because his ears were so big.

He was so unhappy that he decided he would find somewhere else to live, completely on his own.

He travelled for days until he found the perfect place where he settled down for the night.

When he awoke he saw another animal just like him, with even bigger ears. 'What lovely ears,' it said to Big Ears.

No one had told Big Ears that he was supposed to have ears that size — all the other animals that he was related to had them.

But Big Ears had had no parents to tell him that, and now, for the first time in his life, he was really happy.

THE HAPPY PRINCE

There was once a prince who was so popular that when he died, his subjects made a lovely statue of him. It was covered in precious stones.

One day a starling perched on the statue's shoulder and was surprised when the statue whispered to him, 'Take one of my ruby eyes and give it to the poor Widow Frances.'

The bird did as he was told, and every day from then on he took another of the precious stones to a poor citizen. Soon the statue was completely bare and the Chamberlain ordered that it be pulled down. The people were sad, but the starling knew that they would always remember the prince and his statue with love in their hearts. And that would have made the prince very happy indeed.

CHO'S THREE EGGS

Cho was a very poor little Chinese boy who was determined to become rich. All he possessed was a scraggy chicken that his grandmother had given to him. One day he was very surprised to find that the old chicken had laid not one, not two, but three lovely eggs. He was very hungry, but he took the three eggs to the market where he sold them for enough money to buy another chicken.

The next day he had six eggs to sell and with the money he bought two more chickens. The next day all the chickens had laid three eggs each and he had lots of eggs to sell; and that gave him enough money to buy a piglet. All the time the piglet was growing the hens were still laying and Cho kept selling the eggs and buying more chickens and more piglets.

The piglets grew into adult pigs and gave birth to more piglets. And Cho made more and more money until he was the richest farmer in the land.

October **13**

THE SNAKE'S SKIN

There was once a little snake who was forever getting into trouble, so his mother decided one day to tie her tail to his.

But after a day or two, the knot had become so tight that it hurt them both. They pulled and pulled to get themselves free until suddenly they pulled so hard that they slithered right out of their skins. They were so pleased with their new skins that they decided to change them quite often after that, and that's why snakes still shed their skins today.

October **14**

THE TOOTH FAIRY

The Fairy Queen told Bluebell one day that she needed a tooth for a spell and Bluebell was to find it for her.

The excited fairy flew all over the land but could not find a tooth anywhere. Then, when she was just about to fly off home, she looked into a little girl's bedroom. The child was rubbing her face as if she was in pain and then, all of a sudden, she sneezed, and a tooth flew out of her mouth. The little girl smiled and slipped it under her pillow.

Bluebell waited until the child was asleep, flew in and gently removed the tooth. She didn't want anyone to think that she had stolen something so precious, so she left a silver coin in its place.

Some children are still lucky enough

to have Bluebell visit them when they lose a baby tooth. Are you one of them?

October **15**

THE KING'S RIFLE

A king once heard of a wonderful new weapon that was much better than his bows and arrows. He sent his chamberlain to get it for him. It was called a rifle.

When the chamberlain returned with the rifle, the king asked him how it worked. Unfortunately, the chamberlain had forgotten to ask the rifle-maker, so he picked it up by the barrel and whirled it round his head as if it was a club.

'I don't think much of that,' said the king. 'If I'd wanted a club I would have asked for a club.'

And after that he was quite happy with his bows and arrow.

October **16**

JIMMY RUN-RUN

Jimmy used to run everywhere, so everyone called him Jimmy Run-Run.

One night he dreamed that he was running to school as usual, but he could not stop running. He ran straight past the school, out of town and into the country. Nothing could stop him.

The next morning, Jimmy's mother was very surprised when she saw Jimmy walk to school. When he came home she asked him why he'd stopped running.

'I haven't really stopped,' he said. 'I'll still run when I'm late, and for sports, but I noticed an awful lot I'd missed before, like the flowers and the birds and trees.'

'That's very sensible,' said his mother. 'Would you run an errand for me?'

'No, but I'll walk one for you,' laughed Jimmy.

October **17**

MUM'S NEW JOB

Andrew's mother had a new job and had told Andrew to meet her at her workplace after school.

'I don't want to spend my afternoons in an office,' complained Andrew, but his mother insisted. So, later that day Andrew and his three friends went to the office.

Imagine how pleased they were when they found out that Andrew's mother did

that he wanted them to try out. They had a wonderful time, and when the owner asked them to come back the next day they agreed right away. Wouldn't you?

October **18**

SLEEPY STARLIGHT

There was once a fairy called Starlight whose job it was to protect the animals that came out to feed at dusk, just when it was getting dark.

One evening when the sun had set, but there was still just enough light left to see by, a little grey rabbit came out of its burrow to look for something to eat. It was just then that Starlight woke and saw the little creature hopping about, nibbling the grass.

A weasel came out of the woods to look for some supper and saw the rabbit. 'Ah,' it thought, licking its greedy lips, 'here's a tasty morsel for supper.'

not work in an office after all, but in a toyshop.

The owner was pleased when he saw the boys, for he had some new toy guns

But just then a dog ran into the clearing and saw the weasel getting ready to chase the rabbit. The dog began to chase the weasel and Starlight waved her wand just in time. She made the weasel and the dog stop while the rabbit scampered to safety. Then she waved it again and let the dog chase the weasel out of the glade for good.

October **19**

ANDREW'S DAY AT THE FAIR

Andrew's grandmother had been staying with them and on the morning that she left she slipped a pound note into Andrew's hand.

'Don't tell Mummy and Daddy,' she whispered. 'They think I spoil you already.'

Later that morning a fun fair opened on the village green, so Andrew went to collect his friend, Edward, and the two boys set off to have some fun.

They had such a good time. They went on the Helter Skelter, the Waltzer and the Merry-go-round and when it was almost time to go home they had spent most of the money.

Just then they saw a Hoopla stall and Andrew bought five rings. The first one missed, and so did the second and third and fourth, but the fifth one landed over a lovely bottle of perfume which the stall-holder gave them.

'What can we do with perfume?' asked Edward.

'We'll send it to my Granny,' said Andrew. 'After all, if it wasn't for her we wouldn't have had such a nice day.'

So they used the last of the money to buy some stamps and sent the perfume to Granny. Andrew put a little note inside it which read, 'Don't tell Mummy and Daddy, they'll think I'm spoiling you!'

Granny couldn't help feeling very happy when she received the parcel two days later.

October 20

HAZELNUTS

It was a cold, grey day and Susan didn't mind staying indoors, but her mother said that she should go outside. 'Must I?' complained Susan.

'Yes, you must; go and put your coat on, quickly, now.'

'Couldn't we do some cooking instead?' asked Susan.

'Oh, I suppose so,' said Mummy. 'I have got people coming for tea tomorrow and I really ought to bake.'

Susan's mother went to the kitchen and took all the ingredients off the shelves. There was flour, sugar, margarine, chocolate powder . . . but there seemed to be no nuts.

'Don't worry, Mummy,' cried Susan and ran upstairs to collect her coat. She went outside and up the lane. Five minutes later she was back holding some lovely hazelnuts. .. 'I saw them the other day on our walk; don't you remember?'

'You know, I don't think I do,' said Mummy, hiding a packet of nuts behind her back so that Susan wouldn't see that she had had them all the time. She thought that Susan really should get some fresh air that day.

October 21

THE LOST CONTACT LENS

Mr Jones had always worn glasses, for as long as anyone could remember. Suddenly he appeared one day without his spectacles.

'Why, Mr Jones,' said Mrs Livens, his neighbour, 'wherever are your glasses?'

'I've got rid of them,' he replied. 'Don't you think that I'm much better looking without them?'

As he spoke he suddenly tripped over a ball that his dog had been playing with and fell to the ground. As he fell one of the contact lenses tumbled from his eye and landed on the grass, but luckily he found it after a few minutes. He slipped it back into his eye very easily, but suddenly he remembered something that someone had told him a long time ago. Can you think what it could be? That's right. Pride goes before a fall.

October 22

LAZY JACK GOOD-FOR-NOTHING

Jack was, without doubt, the laziest man in the town. All he did every day was lie on his back in the sunshine, snoozing the hours away. No one could ever remember him doing a stroke of work. 'I'll do it tomorrow,' he would say to his wife, who worked hard to make ends meet. She darned his trousers and did her best to mend the house, but it soon became tumble-down and Jack's wife hated living in it. So one morning she packed her bags and left him.

When Jack went home for his lunch, he found a note on the table which said, 'I will come back when you find a job and repair the house.'

'I'll do it tomorrow,' thought Jack.

Tomorrow came and Jack went outside and lay in the sunshine as usual. Suddenly he remembered that he really ought to find a job and begin to mend the roof, but it was such a nice day that Jack thought, 'I'll do it tomorrow.'

When the next day came the same thing happened, and the next and the next . . . Jack never did get round to getting a job and repairing the house, and he never saw his wife again.

Remember, never put off till tomorrow what you can do today.

October 23

SIMON'S NIGHT OUT

One clear, fine night Simon was returning home after dark with his mother. They had been visiting friends and it had got quite late. Simon had never seen the stars look so bright.

'Look!' he cried. 'There's a shooting star. I wish I could catch one and give it to you as a present, Mummy.'

'What a lovely idea, Simon,' said his mother.

When they passed the lake, Simon could hardly believe his eyes, for there in the lake there were lots of stars. 'They must be shooting stars that have fallen in,' he thought to himself.

Later that night he wrapped up in warm clothes and crept out of his room, picked up his fishing rod and went to the lake to try to catch a shooting star.

His mother found him there the next morning and although she pretended to be cross, she was really very pleased that Simon had wanted to catch her a shooting star.

October 24

THE CLEVER FOX

'I'll get that fox,' thought Farmer Jenkins when he realized that a fox had stolen one of his chickens; so he picked up his gun and went out to look for him.

Just as he entered the wood he came across the very fox, leaning against a tree. As soon as he saw Farmer Jenkins with the gun, the fox knew that the farmer was after him.

'Excuse me, Farmer Jenkins,' said the fox. 'I know that it is me you're after, for stealing your chicken. Well, it *was* me and I'm very sorry. My wife and children were so hungry and there was not a berry to be had. So when I saw that you had so many chickens, I'm afraid I took one. I'm sorry and I deserve punishment.'

The farmer was so impressed that he let the fox off, because he had been so honest.

But of course, the fox still stole the farmer's chickens because foxes always do, and he made sure that afterwards he stayed well away from the farmer's woods.

October 25

FARMER JENKINS AGAIN

One day when the fox had stolen another of Farmer Jenkin's chickens, he was determined to catch him and shoot him. He set off into the woods again, but the wily fox was keeping well out of his way.

The farmer searched and searched until he was tired and thirsty. There was not a stream or pond near where he could get water. The poor farmer lay down and went to sleep. He had a very strange dream that a hooded figure was standing over him dropping cool clear water into his mouth, refreshing him. And the strange thing was that when he woke he was no longer thirsty. So he set off for home, giving up all thought of the fox.

What had happened was that the fox has seen the farmer searching for water and had felt so sorry for his old enemy that as the farmer slept he had dropped some water into his mouth.

up into the sky. Soon she could see the moon just ahead of her. All the other crayons were following the green one, but none of them could catch her up. What fun it was.

October 26

TRIP TO THE MOON

Patricia had been in bed for ever so long, with mumps. Now she was out of bed and dressed for the first time; she was sitting by the fire, colouring some pictures, but she was getting very bored.

She left the crayons on the floor and curled up on her favourite chair; her eyelids felt very heavy as she glanced back at her favourite green crayon. It was getting bigger and bigger and bigger and so were all the others.

Suddenly she heard a voice saying, 'Ten. Nine. Eight . . . If you want a ride, Patsy, jump on.' Patricia ran across the room and sat on the green crayon which was now a rocket . . . Two. One. Blast Off. She flew out of the window and up,

168

STOP THIEF

Old Mrs Pratt looked out of her window and saw a ruffian stealing her apples. She pushed open the windows and shouted, 'Stop thief!'

When he ran off, she chased him down the street, shouting 'Stop thief' at the top of her voice.

Everyone ran after the man, but he was too fast for them.

All of a sudden a little dog ran out onto the pavement and the apple thief tripped over it. Before he could get to his feet he was surrounded by his chasers and marched away to the police station.

The dog was patted and petted, but it couldn't really see what all the fuss was about, and it had let the cat it had been chasing get away.

FIRE! FIRE!

What a day it was. Old Mrs Clark was cooking lunch for her husband, when all of a sudden the chip pan caught fire. Now she did what most people would do. She immediately threw water over it and that was completely the wrong thing to do. It made the burning fat splatter and jump all over the place.

The flames spread and soon the whole house was on fire. Mrs Clark just had time to phone the fire brigade before she had to run from the house.

There was a jangle of bells and soon the firemen were there and within a few minutes the blaze was under control.

So if you ever see a chip pan catch fire, don't whatever you do pour water on it. Try to carry it outside very carefully or smother it with something.

October 29

POOR MRS MOUSE

Poor Mrs Mouse was in a dreadful state. She had so many children that she did not know what to do with them. Not only were there so many, they were all in bed with 'flu.

'What shall I do?' she sobbed. 'There's no food in the house and I can't leave them alone and go shopping. They're not well and are crying for me.'

A little bird happened to be flying by and flew off and told all her friends.

In a very short time there was a soft whirring of wings, a gentle buzzing sound and a little knock at Mrs Mouse's front door. Who do you think it was? It was Mrs Bee with a honeycomb, Mrs Butterfly with some butter and Mrs Dragonfly with bread and cakes.

Mrs Mouse was so grateful. She did not know her friends would be so kind. But, as Mrs Bee said, that's what friends are for, after all.

October 30

WHO GOES THERE?

'Halt. Who goes there?' asked the palace guard.

'Clara,' said the young girl standing there. 'But I've left my invitation to the ball at home.'

'You cannot come in then,' said the guard.

Just then the prince came to look for Clara and when he heard what had hap-

pened he was very angry with the guard.

'He was just doing his job,' said Clara. 'Please don't be cross with him. You should reward him, rather than punish him.'

So the prince gave the soldier a bag of gold and thanked him for doing his job so well.

It's no wonder that when she married the prince some time later, Clara was the most popular princess who had ever ruled the land.

October 31

THE BRAVE SHEEPDOG

One day when his master had gone for lunch, Bob the Sheepdog was left in charge of the flock.

All of a sudden a man appeared. Bob recognized him immediately. The last time the shepherd had taken him into town, Bob had seen the man's face on a poster outside the police station. He was a wanted sheep stealer.

Bob ran straight off into the town. He went into the police station and barked and barked so loudly that the policemen knew that he was trying to tell them something. When Bob ran out of the station, the policemen followed him right back to the farm where the criminal was rounding up the sheep.

Bob's master was very pleased when the thief was arrested and gave him a specially juicy bone for supper that night.

November 1

HOW JONATHAN MARRIED A PRINCESS

Once upon a time there was a kingdom and its royal palace was built on a steep rock. The king of that country had a very clever daughter who declared that she would only marry a man who made her say, 'That can't be true.'

Noblemen came from far and wide and told her the most outrageous things but none of them could make her say, 'It can't be true.'

One day a farmer's son, called Jonathan, had an idea and made his way to the royal palace. He was shown into the throne room where the princess was sitting.

'Your Royal Highness,' he began, bowing low, 'I must tell you about an amazing adventure I had. It was like this . . . but before I begin — do you know that you have a dirty mark on your face?'

The princess's hand flew to her face. 'That can't be true, I washed it very carefully . . .'

She then realized that she had been tricked. But true to her word she married the farmer's son and grew to love him very much, for he was just as clever as she was.

November 2

THE WITCH

There was once a lonely witch whom no one ever talked to because she was so wicked.

'I can't help being wicked,' she said to everyone. 'I was born that way.'

But it was no good. No one ever talked to her and she became lonelier and lonelier.

One day she thought to herself that maybe if she tried to be less wicked, then people would be nicer too. So next morning she went into the town and did all sorts of nice things. She helped old ladies to cross the road. She carried shopping bags and weeded gardens.

By the end of the day everyone knew that the witch had turned over a new leaf and she soon had so many friends that she was never lonely again.

November 3

THE HAPPY SHEPHERD

All the sheep loved their shepherd and he knew every one of them by their own name. One day he did not turn up and a surly old man came in his place.

'The shepherd is very ill,' the sheepdog told the sheep. 'The doctor does not think that he'll live much longer.'

That night when the surly shepherd had gone home, all the sheep made their way to the old shepherd's house and gathered around his window baaing softly.

The shepherd heard them and real-ized how much they would miss him if he died. From that moment on he began to get well and a few weeks later was back at work again with his sheep.

November 4

THE THREE APPLES

There were three apples on the kitchen table and just as Emma and Nick were about to eat one each, their mother came into the kitchen and gave them such a row that they hid from her until lunch-time.

They played quietly in the garden, keeping out of Mummy's way, wondering why she had been so cross.

At lunch when they had finished their meat and potatoes, Mummy gave them a toffee apple each for pudding. 'That's why I was so cross,' she explained. 'I wanted to make toffee apples and I only had three apples left. And I wanted one for myself.'

As soon as they finished they ran upstairs and brushed their teeth and went out to play until teatime.

November 5

CROCODILE TEARS

'What's the matter with you, Chloe?' the zookeeper asked the crocodile one day.

'It's my birthday and no one's remembered it. Not even a miserable card,' sobbed Chloe.

'Oh, is that all?' said the zookeeper.

'Oh, is that all,' cried Chloe after him. 'Not even so much as a "Happy Birthday" from him.'

An hour later there was a great commotion and all the animals came into the enclosure with the keeper. They were all carrying brightly wrapped presents, and they all gathered round Chloe and sang 'Happy Birthday to you'.

'We thought we'd surprise you and have a birthday party for you when the zoo was closed,' said the tiger.

And that's exactly what they did — and they had a marvellous time.

November 6

THE HANDSOME SOLDIER

A handsome soldier rode into town one day and he was looking for an adventure.

'There's no adventure here,' everyone said. 'Nothing ever happens.'

'Surely there must be adventures sometime,' the soldier replied.

'Never,' everyone said.

Just then a man with a large sack ran out of the bank. He was followed by the bank manager, who shouted, 'Stop thief!'

'Leave this to me,' shouted the soldier and rode off after the thief. A few seconds later he had caught the thief and he was soon safely locked up in jail.

'I thought you said nothing ever happened,' said the soldier.

'It doesn't usually,' said the bank manager. 'It's just as well you were here when something did happen, isn't it?'

'I'd better stay here just in case I'm needed again,' said the soldier. But nothing ever happened again.

November **7**

THE FORGOTTEN GLOVE

Once upon a time there was a lady who was in such a hurry one day that she ran

out of her house and picked up only one glove from her table. She was in her carriage when she discovered her dreadful mistake, but she could not go back for her glove because she was so late.

There was only one thing to do. She put on her one glove and went to her party.

Everyone stared at her one glove, but the lady carried on charmingly.

She was very relieved when she could go home.

The next day she went to another party and was astonished to see all the ladies were wearing only one glove.

What had happened was that everyone at the party the day before thought that the lady with the one glove had left her other hand ungloved intentionally and was starting a new fashion. And that's just what happened. For the rest of that year no one was ever seen with two gloves at any smart party. All because of the lady who forgot her glove one day.

November **8**

SIR GARETH AND THE MAIDEN

A long time ago there were knights who were famous for their brave and daring deeds. One of the bravest of all was Sir Gareth.

One day he was riding home when he heard a girl screaming in the distance. 'Help. Oh please help,' she cried.

Sir Gareth spurred his horse and galloped off to the rescue. When he got to where the voice was coming from he was horrified to see that a beautiful girl was being dragged away by a horrible ogre. But Sir Gareth was not afraid.

With his sword he slashed the ogre's foot and the pain was so great that the ogre dropped the maiden and bent down to stop the bleeding. As the ogre bent, Sir Gareth stabbed him in the hand. The ogre fell to his knees because the pain was so intense. Sir Gareth gathered all his strength and chopped the ogre's head off.

The maiden was so beautiful that Sir Gareth immediately fell in love with her. The two were married that very day and lived happily ever after.

November **9**

THE WOODPECKER

Paul was a little boy who lived in a big city with his parents. One day his grandmother asked him to go and stay with her in the country for a whole week.

When Mummy drove off he felt a little lonely as he waved goodbye to her. Suddenly he caught sight of a lovely coloured bird sitting in a tree in Granny's garden.

'Look, Granny,' he cried. 'What a lovely parrot!'

'No, dear,' Granny smiled. 'It's a woodpecker. It comes here every day to be fed.'

'May I feed it?' Paul said; so Granny went inside and a few minutes later came out with nuts and chopped fruit. Paul took some in his hand and held it out. The woodpecker flew down from its branch and landed on Paul's wrist and gratefully ate all the food.

Suddenly Paul didn't feel so lonely any more. The week flew by and Paul had so much to tell Mummy when she came to collect him that he was a bit sad at leaving Granny. But Granny said he could come back again soon. She was going to miss him, and so would the woodpecker.

November **10**

THE WIZARD'S CAT

Waldo was a wicked wizard who could do all sorts of magic tricks. He could turn himself into a bird and fly high in the air. He could turn himself into a fish and swim in the stream. He had a cat which he treated very badly. He never fed it and often locked it away for days on end.

One day the cat said to its master, 'I've seen you turn yourself into a bird and a fish. But I've never seen you turn yourself a into lion. I bet you can't.'

The wizard said some magic words and in an instant became a roaring lion. The terrified cat ran up the curtains, it was so afraid.

'Very good,' it said from its safe place.

'But I bet you can't turn yourself into a mouse.'

The roaring lion instantly became a little mouse, scampering around the room.

Before you could blink an eye the cat jumped down from the curtain rail and killed the wicked wizard.

November **11**

HARRY THE MOUSE MOVES HOUSE

Harry the Mouse had spent all summer

in a corner of an old garden shed, but now the nights were getting quite cold, so he decided to find a warmer place to live.

He ran into the house when no one was looking and up into the attic. He had a lovely time looking into all the old boxes and furniture that had been left up there.

Suddenly he came across a funny box that had a sort of dome on top and a handle which he could push round — and a little drawer underneath.

'This would make an ideal house,' Harry squeaked happily. 'I can put my stores under the roof and sleep in the bedroom underneath and when I am bored I can play on the roundabout.'

He collected all his belongings from the garden shed and slipped back up to the attic.

Can you think what his new house really was? It was an old coffee mill.

November **12**

HORSE FOR SALE

Poor Johnny had two things left in the world—his horse and a basket of lettuce seeds. To pay the rent, he decided he would have to sell them.

He stood by the roadside one day and offered passers-by his last two possessions. No one payed any attention until an old man passed and asked him why he was selling the horse and lettuce seeds. When Johnny explained the old man said, 'Why don't you plant the lettuce seeds and sell the lettuces when they grow, and to pay the rent, why not hire the horse out for rides? All the children like riding, but few of them can afford their own horses.'

Johnny thought for a moment or two and then agreed with the old man. He went back to the cottage he lived in and painted a big sign saying, 'HORSE RIDING HERE'.

Within a few days he had earned enough money to pay the rent. And when the lettuce seeds grew he sold the lettuces for enough money to buy lots more seeds which he planted in his garden.

November 13

SAM THE SEAL

One day a big ship sailed past the ice where Sammy the Seal lived. Sammy saw a small boat being let down into the sea and a few moments later a man appeared on the ice with a camera and took photographs of the seal.

Now Sammy was never to know this, but when the photographer went home, the film was developed and the photograph of Sammy was used to advertise a new brand of soap powder called Seal. Pictures of Sammy were everywhere—on buses, underground stations, railway stations, even on television. Sammy became a household name.

November 14

THE FAIRY OF THE LOCH

Loch is a Scottish word for lake and this story is about a Scottish fairy who lived beside a loch.

One winter's night she went to visit another fairy on the other side of the loch. It was getting late as she left her friend and made her way home. It was almost sunrise and she had to get home before then, because if a ray of sunlight touched her she knew she would be turned into a flower. She looked up into the sky and made a wish. 'I wish,' she thought, 'that the last star in the sky could swoop down and carry me home before sunrise.'

Now fortunately the Queen of the Fairies heard her wish. The Fairy of the Loch was a particular favourite of the queen's and she immediately granted her wish.

Almost before the Fairy of the Loch had stopped wishing, the last star in the sky swooped down and carried her safely home.

Next time you look up into the sky and see a star swooping across it, maybe

it's the same star that the Queen of the Fairies sent for the Fairy of the Loch. Maybe it is carrying another fairy home before the sun rises.

November **15**

THE EMPEROR PENGUINS

Once penguins were all the same, but one day a very brave penguin saved all the other penguins from disaster. A crew of pirates sailed into the icy bay where they lived, began to chase the birds and took them on board their ship. The brave penguin managed to hide from the pirates, and when darkness fell and the men were in their cabins, he slipped on board their ship and unlocked the cages where his brothers and sisters and friends were being held.

Once everyone was safely ashore, the brave penguin untied the ropes that anchored the ship and all the penguins swam up behind the ship and pushed and pushed until the ship was far away from the shore. With no anchor on board the pirates couldn't stop the ship floating away until it ran aground thousands of miles away.

The penguins were so pleased with the brave penguin that they decided to make him their emperor. The other penguins knew that if trouble ever threatened again the emperor penguin's chicks would rescue them, so the chicks and later their chicks were all made emperor penguins. Today there are still emperor penguins in the Antarctic.

was not a cloud in the sky, and the sun shone brightly for the rest of the day.

The next morning when Sheila woke up the sun was shining through her windows. 'You gave me such a fright yesterday,' said Sheila. And the sun seemed to wink at her as if to say he had only been teasing her.

November 17

THE ASS, THE COCK AND THE LION

An ass and a cock once lived on the same farm very happily together. But one day a hungry lion happened to pass the farm, and when it saw the plump ass, it decided that it would have the beast for its supper.

Just at that moment the cock crowed and as soon as the lion heard the cock's crow, it ran off as quickly as possible.

The ass thought it was very funny to see the mighty lion run away from the sound of a cockerel crowing, and boldly galloped after the lion, jeering at it as it ran.

But as soon as the lion was out of earshot, it turned round and with one mighty blow of a paw, it killed the ass and ate it. The cockerel was upset at the death of his good friend, but then he realized that it was really the ass's fault; he had been too confident, and false confidence is very often the forerunner of misfortune.

November 16

SUNSHINE SHEILA

Sheila was one of the lucky people on whom the sun always seems to shine. One day her teacher decided to take the whole class on an outing.

'It's lucky for us that Sheila's in the class,' said the teacher. 'It's bound to be sunny for our outing because the sun always shines on Sheila.'

The day was chosen and all the children began to get very excited. Sheila decided to have a word with the sun and tell him that he had to shine on the day. But every day for a whole week before the outing the sun did not shine.

On the morning of the outing Sheila's mother said, 'You'd better tell your friends to take their raincoats.'

Sheila was disappointed. As they drove through the countryside it got gloomier and gloomier, but all of a sudden the clouds parted and the sun began to shine. By the time they had reached the place they were to have lunch, there

---

November 18

UNCLE CHARLEY

Uncle Charley was a conjurer. He often

181

went to children's parties and entertained the children there.

One day, John-John was having a party and Uncle Charley came as usual. He did all the usual tricks. He made rabbits come out of his funny hat and then he did the best trick of all. He asked John-John to come and stand beside him. When the boy did as he had been asked, Uncle Charley said some magic words and waved his hands over John-John's head. Suddenly the boy disappeared. All his friends gasped in astonishment.

Then John-John suddenly came back again, after Uncle Charley said some more magic words.

'Where have you been?' cried John-John's friends.

'Nowhere!' said John-John.

'But you disappeared,' they all shouted. 'Uncle Charley made you disappear.'

'Did you, Uncle Charley?' asked John-John.

'Yes, I did,' said the magician.

'How?' all the boys and girls asked.

But Uncle Charley would only say, 'That's my secret, isn't it?'

November **19**

THE VERY FIRST GOLDFISH

There was once a great famine in the Valley of the Rising Sun. One day a little girl who lived there wrote a letter and sent it to a prince who lived in a far-off land, where the same river that ran through the Valley of the Rising Sun also flowed. She told him all about their troubles. She painted one of her pet fish bright gold and tied the letter to it.

The fish swam and swam and was eventually caught by a fisherman who

proud man that in another part of the kingdom a young man had a curlier beard.

Now Hassam was furious. But what could he do? Everyone in the land had beards and if this young man's beard was going to grow curlier than his then there was nothing he could do.

Suddenly he had a brainwave. 'I shall tell all my subjects to cut their beards off.' He told his smiths to make thin sharp blades and give them to all the men to cut their beards with every morning. And that's how razor blades came into the world.

November 21

KARIM, THE SILLY BAKER'S BOY

In Arabia, a long time ago, there was a baker's boy called Karim, who was as lazy as lazy could be.

One day his master had to go out of town and he told Karim to bake the bread that was needed for that day.

Karim set to work slowly and as soon as the loaves were in the oven, he sat down and promptly fell asleep.

He was awakened a few hours later by the smell of burning bread. He took the loaves out of the oven and was horrified when he saw black burn marks on all of them.

He couldn't be bothered baking any more, so he scraped off the burned bits and delivered the bread to the waiting customers.

His master was very pleased when he came back and saw that all the bread had been delivered. However when he went out his customers were furious.

sent it to the prince, along with the letter. The prince was so pleased with the lovely gold fish that he sent lots of rice to the girl.

The little girl was so grateful that she sent the prince another gold-painted fish. The prince put it in a tank along with the first one and when the two fish mated and had little fish, the baby fish were gold, too. And that's how goldfish came into the world.

November 20

THE MAGIC MIRROR

'Who has the curliest beard of all?' Hassam asked his mirror every morning, and the mirror always answered, 'Master of the world, most feared, you have, by far, the curliest beard.'

One day, however, the mirror told the

They threw the loaves at the baker and told him that they were hard and uneatable.

The baker rushed home and found Karim asleep. He thrashed him soundly and made him pay for the wasted bread. After that Karim had all the time in the world to be lazy, for his master fired him as soon as the bread was paid for—which served Karim right.

November **22**

GRANDDAD'S NEW SHOES

Peter's grandfather never used to go out in the wintertime when it was slippery underfoot.

'I'd like to go out,' he used to say to Peter, 'but I may fall and hurt myself.'

And so the old man used to sit unhap-

pily indoors for most of the winter until spring came again.

One year Peter had a brainwave. He took a pair of his grandfather's boots to the cobbler and asked him to put special non-slip rubber soles on them.

A few days later it was grandfather's birthday, and when Peter went to visit him the old man looked very glum when he saw that all Peter had brought was an old pair of boots.

'Let's go out for a walk, Grandpa,' said Peter.

'You know I can't,' grumbled the old man. 'I'll fall over.'

'Not with these new soles on the boots,' said Peter.

The old man put the boots on and went outside with Peter. They walked for miles and neither of them slipped once on the icy roads.

It was the best present grandfather had had for years.

THE HEN AND THE FOX

A fox was once out looking for a late supper. He came to a henhouse and through the open door he could see a hen, high up on its perch, safely out of his reach.

'Here,' thought the fox, 'is a challenge to my persuasive powers.' After thinking for some time he called out to the hen, 'Hello, friend hen, have you been ill? I haven't seen you around recently. I was very worried about you when I heard someone say you had been off colour. You do look a bit pale, you know.'

The hen ignored the fox.

'If you step down,' continued the fox, 'I'll take your pulse and look after you.'

'I don't think I ought to,' said the hen. 'If I climb down, it's not my pulse you

will take, I think you'll take my life, too, for you look very hungry.'

The fox slunk away. He didn't know that the hen had been warned against insincere friends.

THE ODD CLUB

'What an odd looking club,' thought Franz the hunter as he walked through the forest one day and spotted the knobbly stick lying at his feet. He bent down and picked it up. As soon as he had done so a little goblin appeared and asked him to make two wishes.

'I wish I had long fair hair,' said Franz, who was as bald as a coot. Imme-

diately his hair grew and grew until it was so long he had to tie it in plaits.

Just then his friend Hans passed by, and as soon as he saw Franz he burst out laughing.

'How silly you look,' he giggled. 'Men shouldn't wear their hair like that,' and he walked on.

Franz picked up the club again and the goblin reappeared. 'What do you want now?' it said.

'I want to be bald again,' pleaded Franz.

'Yes, you do look a bit silly like that,' said the goblin and made Franz bald again. He felt much less silly.

November **25**

THE THREE ROBBERS

There were once three robbers who stole a large bag of gold from a bank one day. They carried it far from town and when night came they were very tired and lay down to rest.

'I'm not going to go to sleep,' said the first robber. 'If I do you two will run off with the gold.'

'I'm not either,' said the second.

'I trust you both,' said the third and promptly fell asleep, or so the other two thought.

'How silly we both are not to trust each other,' the two robbers agreed and began to nod off.

But the third robber had only been pretending, and as soon as he knew that the others were fast asleep he·woke up and quietly tiptoed off with the gold.

When the two awoke, they were horri-

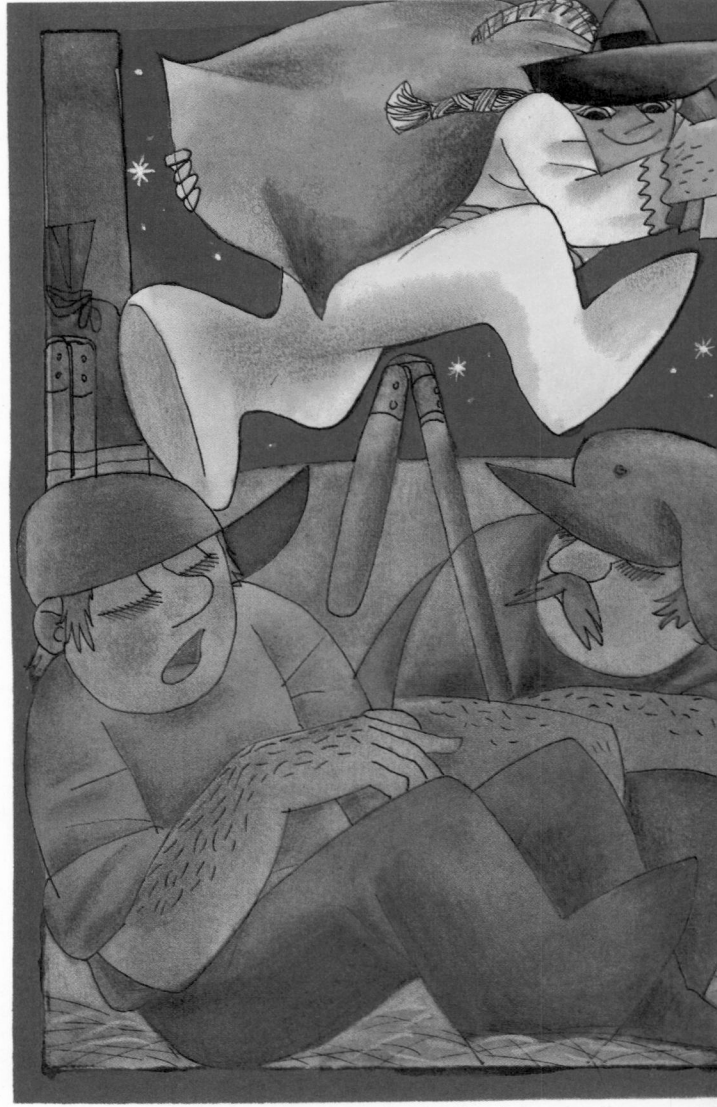

fied at what had happened. 'It is true, isn't it?' said the first robber. 'There is no honour among thieves.'

And the second nodded sadly in agreement.

November **26**

THE ANGRY GIANT

The townsfolk of Salovia were terrified of the giant who lived nearby, and of his pet eagle.

Once every month they came into town and the giant was so angry when everyone hid from him that he did spiteful things, like pull up trees from the ground.

'Why will no one talk to us?' the giant asked the eagle one day.

'Maybe if we gave them something to show that we're not really as bad as they think, they would like us more,' said the eagle.

They went home and prepared a beautiful meal. The next morning they packed it into hampers and carried them into town where they spread it out on a long table in the village square.

The eagle flew all over town and asked everyone to the banquet. At first everyone was afraid, but soon their curiosity got the better of them and one by one they crept out of their houses and began to eat the food. The giant was

happy that they were all enjoying themselves and from then on he was always a welcome visitor when he came to town.

November **27**

OLD DAISY

Farmer Giles had bought a fine new tractor to help him plough the land around his farmhouse.

But he kept on Old Daisy, the horse that had pulled the plough in his father's day.

Then one morning the tractor broke down and the mechanic said that it could not be repaired for a month, long after the ploughing season was over.

The farmer was in despair because he had to do the ploughing right away. So he harnessed Old Daisy to the old plough, and the old horse was so glad to be useful again that he ploughed the field in almost the same time as it would have taken with the tractor. The farmer was so pleased that after that he often allowed Old Daisy to pull the plough.

November **28**

A COLD CURE

There was once a chef who had a very strange dream. He dreamed that he had a portrait and one night the man in the picture caught cold. He told the chef to make him a hot drink and the chef did as he was asked. He took it to the man who drank it down and immediately felt better.

The next morning the chef felt dread-

187

ful. His eyes were running, his nose was blocked up and he couldn't stop coughing.

He remembered the drink in his dream and told his wife to go and make it for him. She did as she was asked and brought her husband a steaming mug of the brew a few minutes later. The chef drank it down but felt no different.

'Are you sure you made it properly?' he asked his wife.

'Yes. It was a very odd recipe. Where on earth did you get it?'

'I dreamed it last night.'

'You silly. Dreams like that don't come true you know. Now you'll just stay in bed until your cold's gone. That's the only thing to do with a cold.'

And she was right.

November **29**

THE RICH MAN AND HIS WIFE

Once upon a time a very rich man and woman lived in Spain. They were so rich that they owned all the land as far as the eye could see in any direction.

One day they went out for a walk and came across two ragged children. They were laughing and smiling and having a happy time.

'How can you two be so happy and yet be so poor?' the man asked.

'Poor! How can anyone be poor on a day like this? The sun is shining and everything is so beautiful. What does money matter?' said the boy.

'And anyway, we have lots of friends,' said the girl.

'Especially each other,' said the boy.

'We don't have any friends,' the lady said to her husband.

'That's because you're so grand. And people are afraid of you, because you're rich,' the boy said.

The rich pair went home and thought long and hard. 'I think I'd rather have friends than eat off gold plates and live like this,' said the man, and his wife agreed.

So the very next day they gave all their possessions away and do you know what? They felt so happy and soon they had a lot of friends and they lived out their days in great contentment.

November **30**

JOHNNY'S GAME

When Johnny was a little boy he made a wonderful discovery. He found out that if he pressed the little button on the front door, a bell rang inside the house and Mummy came dashing out.

That made Johnny very happy. If he was playing in the garden and wanted to speak to Mummy, he pressed the bell.

Sometimes he would slip out and press the bell. It was great fun to hear the ringing noises and watch Mummy run down the hall. Why didn't Mummy think so too, he asked her one day.

'Because I think that if the bell rings it must be the milkman or gasman and I rush down and there's nobody there.'

'Nobody?' said Johnny indignantly. 'I'm there.'

'Yes, I know, darling, but if you want to say something to me why don't you come and see me.'

'That's not so much fun,' thought Johnny. But Mummy looked so serious when she said it that he didn't press the bell again—at least, not very often.

THE KING WITH BIG FEET

There was once a king who had enormous feet and his subjects called him King Big Feet, although his real name was Rupert. One day King Big Feet said aloud, 'I wish I had ordinary feet.'

A fairy happened to be passing and heard his wish. She flew into the palace and said, 'If you really want ordinary feet you could have them. But you would have to give the fairies your eldest daughter in exchange.'

The king was very fond of his eldest daughter, but he looked down at his

feet and felt sure that she would understand. He summoned her to the throne room and explained that he was going to give her to the fairies in exchange for a pair of ordinary feet.

'But Father,' the princess cried. 'You wouldn't be the same with ordinary feet.'

'What do you mean?' asked the king.

'You are a good king. Your subjects love you. It doesn't matter a jot to them that you have big feet.'

'You mean that they don't laugh at me because of my feet.'

'Laugh at you! Heavens, no.'

The king was so pleased at this that he sent the fairy away and never bothered about his feet ever again.

December **2**

GRANNY COMES TO STAY

Rob's grandmother was an old lady, very old indeed. She used to live on her own, but one day Rob's mother told him that she couldn't live on her own any more and that she was coming to live with them.

'Here!' cried Rob. 'I don't want her here. She's so old.' 'Don't be silly, Rob. She's coming and that's that.'

A few days later, the old lady moved in. Rob was still so cross that he refused to talk to her.

One day, Rob caught a dreadful cold and had to stay in bed. He was tucked up in bed when there was a knock on his door. 'Come in,' called Rob.

Rob's grandmother came in and sat down on a chair beside his bed.

'You know when I was little and had

a cold my grandmother used to tell me lovely stories. Would you like to hear some of her tales?'

'I suppose so,' said Rob grumpily.

Granny told him wonderful stories and when she had finished she said, 'I know a lot more. I could tell you one every night if you like.'

Rob said that, Yes, he would love it and every night after that Granny came to his room and told him a story.

December **3**

JOLLY ROBIN REDBREAST

Once, many years ago a beautiful princess lived in a castle. She had two little brown birds that she kept as pets.

One sad day the princess's lands were invaded. Her castle was surrounded by soldiers who fired arrows into her room. The princess hid behind a chest. After a fierce battle her troops forced back the enemy, but one enemy soldier managed to shoot two arrows from his bow, just as he was fleeing. The princess had thought it was safe to come out of her hiding place, and her two birds watched horrified as the arrows flew towards her heart. Without thinking they flew down and let the arrows pierce them to save the princess. As they lay on the floor with their breasts covered in blood, the princess wept and her tears fell on the birds. Miraculously they came to life again, but from that day all birds like them have had bright red breasts.

December **4**

TICK TOCK

Tick Tock was an old clock that stood on a shelf with an old vase, a cup and some other useless things. Tick Tock was useless because a long time ago someone had lost the key that wound him up and his hands had long since stopped.

One day an old lady came into the shop where he lived and bought him for a few pennies.

She took him home and cleaned him up and put him on her mantleshelf. And then she opened a drawer and Tick Tock could see lots of clock keys. Tick Tock did not know it but the old lady's father had been a collector of keys and she was sure that amongst the collection there must be one to fit Tick Tock.

And she was right. The second key she tried wound him up perfectly. And when his big hand reached six, he chimed the half hour loudly.

December **5**

THE APPLE COMPETITION

'Whosoever names the apple which my daughter the Princess Melody has cultivated shall win her hand in marriage,' King Florimund announced one day.

All the courtiers suggested names but the king liked none of them. And then, all of a sudden, the kitchen boy suggested a name. Now he was the handsomest man in the palace and the princess had never seen him before, because he was a kitchen boy. As soon as her eyes fell on him she immediately fell in love with him and was happy when her father decided that the name he had suggested was quite perfect. The happy couple were married the next day and lived happily ever after. Of course, the king had to make the kitchen boy a prince, but that was easily arranged; after all he was king and could do what he liked.

December **6**

THE SHORT-SIGHTED CROW

It was very cold and the ground was

covered with thick, slippery snow, so slippery that when Ronnie went out to make a snowman, he fell flat on his back. But he wasn't hurt, thank goodness.

He spent all morning making a snowman and a very odd looking one it was too. When it was finished Ronnie gave him a broom to hold and put a bucket on his head for a hat. He also decided to give the snowman two pairs of glasses.

When Ronnie went indoors to have lunch a short-sighted crow flew by. Because he was short-sighted he did not see the snowman and flew straight into it with such a thump that one of the pairs of glasses fell to the ground. The crow picked up the glasses and tried them on. Immediately he could see perfectly, so he decided to keep them. He flew off and Ronnie was most puzzled when he came out and couldn't find the spectacles anywhere. He's still puzzled to this day.

December **7**

MARY'S GARDEN

Mary lived in a flat with her mother and father. She loved the building and the people who lived in it very much, but there was one thing she really wanted but could not have. It was a garden.

She would love to have spent time weeding and planting and watching plants and flowers grow and come to life. But you can't have a garden in a flat. Or can you? One day Mary's aunt and uncle came to visit from Australia. They gave Mary's parents some lovely presents and then gave Mary a large package. When Mary unwrapped it she found a large box, a little spade, potting compost and some little packets.

'What is it?' cried Mary.

'It's a window box,' said Mary's aunt.

'Daddy will fix it to the ledge outside your bedroom window and you can fill it with the compost and plant the seeds.'

Mary couldn't wait to begin gardening. And when the box was fitted she had a wonderful time in her own little garden.

SPOT SAVES THE DAY

Spot belonged to a little boy called Paul.

One day Paul took Spot to the shops with him and tied him up outside when he went in to buy some sweets.

The street was completely empty and only Spot saw the man force open a window in a house across the road and climb in.

Spot began to bark and bark. Paul and the shop-keeper ran out to see what all the commotion was about.

As soon as Spot was let off his lead he dashed across the road and, staring up at the window that had been broken, he began to bark and bark and bark.

Paul realized that something odd must have happened and ran back to the shop to call the police.

A few minutes later the burglar was safely under lock and key and all because Spot had been such a vigilant dog. Well done, Spot!

December 9

TOMMY'S BABYSITTER

Tommy's mummy and daddy were going out for the evening and Miss Brown was going to babysit.

'You won't be any trouble, will you, Tommy?' said Mummy.

As soon as Mummy and Daddy had gone out, it was bathtime. Nothing Miss Brown could do would stop Tommy splashing. He made such a mess that Miss Brown had to mop up and while she was doing that Tommy put on his pyjamas and went downstairs.

He decided to make himself a sandwich and made such a mess that as soon as Miss Brown had cleaned up the bathroom, she had to clean up the kitchen.

The poor lady was so tired that as she was reading Tommy a bedtime story she fell asleep.

Imagine how surprised Tommy's parents were when they came home and found Tommy watching television and Miss Brown sound asleep in Tommy's bed.

December 10

THE SAD CLOWN

Coco the Clown was very sad. His friend Pepo, another clown, had moved away and he had no one to do his act with.

He was so sad that he sat down and cried. Just then his cat, Crystal, padded over to him and put a comforting paw on his knee.

'Can't I help?' it seemed to be saying. Coco looked at the cat and thought, 'If I dressed you up in a funny costume and put a mask on you, we could do a good act together.'

He did just that and practised for weeks and weeks and eventually the act was ready. Both Coco and Crystal were very nervous as they waited in the wings and heard the ringmaster announce the new act. But they need not have worried. They had practised so hard and were so funny that they were a great success—the best in the show!

December 11

A PONY FOR SANDRA

Sandra was crazy about horses, but her parents could not possibly afford to buy her a pony of her own.

She had hundreds of books on horses and whenever there was a programme about horses on television she sat glued to the set.

One Saturday, Sandra's father asked her if she would like to go for a run in the country. They had not driven very far when he stopped the car and told Sandra to get out.

They were outside a stable. Sandra's father took her hand and led her inside.

'Here she is,' he said to the lady who came to greet them.

'Oh good,' she said, 'I could do with the extra help.'

Sandra's father had arranged for Sandra to help in the stables every Saturday from then on.

Sandra was the happiest girl in the world.

December 12

THE FAIRY'S DRESS

Many, many years ago a fairy wanted to make a white dress for a moonlight ball. But there was nothing pure white to make the dress with. Where could she find something?

All of a sudden she had an idea. She carried some eiderdowns from the queen's palace up to the roof and took out all the feathers. Then she blew her magic whistle to call the cold north wind. It came immediately, blowing the feathers in swirling clouds down onto the earth below, where they became pure white snowflakes. Then she emptied a sack of diamond dust and summoned the east wind. It came immediately and blew all over the snow, turning it into

sparkling frost. The fairy made her dress out of the crisp snow, sparkling with frost, and it was the most beautiful dress at the ball.

December 13

THE SLEEPY SENTRY

Richard Valiant was the most popular outlaw in the land. He stole from the rich and gave everything to the poor.

Alas, one day he was caught and thrown into jail. He was put under the care of Captain Vigilant, who sat outside Richard's cell for hour after hour, never taking a break.

Now remember that Richard was one of the cleverest men in the land. One of the things that he had learned to do was to hypnotize people.

He began to swing his gold watch chain backwards and forwards and the captain could not take his eyes off it. Richard began to tell the captain that he was feeling tired and the captain began to feel tired. After a few moments Richard told the captain to unlock the door and set him free. The poor soldier was so deeply under Richard's hypnotic power that he obeyed his commands.

By the time he woke up, Richard was miles and miles away in safe hiding and the captain had an awful lot of explaining to do.

December **14**

BAKING DAY

Mrs Bear was baking special bread today. Usually she made ordinary bread that her children loved to eat warm from the oven, with lashings of butter running all over it. But today she was being very secretive. She told the children to leave the kitchen while she mixed the special dough.

The children were disappointed because they loved helping their mother on baking day. They stood looking very dejected outside. Suddenly little Willie said, 'Let's climb up on the dustbin and watch Mummy bake.' And that's what they did.

They watched as Mummy mixed the dough, but it was different dough than usual. There was butter and sugar and treacle in it. And nuts and chopped fruit and spices. When it was ready, she popped it in the oven and the children went off to play.

'I wonder what it was,' said Willie.

'It wasn't the usual bread at all,' said Angus, his brother. When they went back into the kitchen Mummy was putting the baking into a big tin. It smelt delicious. On the tin there was a big notice saying NOT TO BE OPENED UNTIL THE 25TH DECEMBER.

Can you guess what was in the tin?

December **15**

MANDY'S FLOWERS

'I wish we could have flowers in the house, but they are so expensive at this time of year,' Mandy's mother had said last year. And Mandy was determined that the next year she would find winter flowers for her mother.

In the springtime she collected lovely violets, beautiful blue forget-me-nots and pale yellow primroses. She put them between two pieces of paper under a heavy book.

In the summertime, just before harvest, she picked bright red poppies and some corn from the field. She put them under the book beside the spring flow-

ers. And then she went and picked some dried grass and pretty autumn-coloured leaves and did the same with them.

In winter when her mother was wishing she could have winter flowers, Mandy gave her the dried, pressed flowers and grasses and leaves that she had collected and her mother was so happy that she almost cried.

December **16**

THE SLEEPING BEAUTY

Once upon a time a prince was lost in a forest. Suddenly he came to a clearing and saw a castle in the distance.

He rode up to the gates and was astonished to find that the guards were sound asleep.

He went past them into the courtyard. There were several servants there, all stretched out on the ground, sound asleep. It was the same inside. Everywhere he went there were sleeping servants and courtiers.

He made his way into the throne room and there, on their thrones, were the king and queen, snoring loudly.

There was a door open off the throne room and through it the prince could see a beautiful girl lying on a silk-covered bed, as soundly asleep as everyone else.

She was so lovely that the prince felt that he had to kiss her, and when he did what do you think happened?

I think I'll tell you tomorrow.

December **17**

THE PRINCESS AWAKENS

As soon as the prince's lips touched the lips of the princess, she awoke.

The prince asked her what had happened. She told him that when she had

been christened, her parents had asked all the fairies to come to the party, but they had forgotten to ask the wicked Carabousse. When she heard about the christening, the wicked witch was furious and cast a spell on the princess. On her sixteenth birthday, she said, the princess would prick her finger on a spindle and would fall asleep along with everyone in the palace. It happened exactly as the witch had foretold. And the princess would only awake when she was kissed by a prince whom she would marry.

'Will you marry me?' asked the prince, and gave her the only token of love he had with him, which was a lovely apple as sweet and pure and beautiful as his love. The princess agreed and they lived happily ever after.

December 18

MUMMY'S BIRTHDAY CARD

It was Mummy's birthday and Peggy had been out with Grandma to buy her a present. But Peggy wanted to give Mummy something else that she had made all by herself with no grown-up help at all. So she decided to paint Mummy a birthday card.

She took all her paints and painted a picture of a lovely green holly bush with red berries on it.

Peggy thought that it was a very good picture — a little smudgy perhaps but, as she had heard Mummy say to Daddy very often, nothing is always perfect, especially when her cooking had gone a little wrong.

Then she remembered that cards ought to have writing on them. This was a bit difficult as Peggy could not really write very well, yet. But she tried very hard and wrote 'HAPPY BIRTHDAY MUMMY' on it. Only it really read, 'HAPY BIRFDAE MUMI', but it didn't matter at all.

December **19**

THE CHRISTMAS TREE

Just before Christmas one year some evil thieves broke into a castle and stole all the decorations and all the presents. Everyone was very sad.

But Hamish crept out of the castle into the forest where he chopped down the greenest tree he could find.

He pulled the tree back to the castle and hid it in his room. All that night he made decorations out of everything he

could find and painted them gold and silver.

He then found lots of tiny candles and attached them to the tree. The next morning when everyone came down to breakfast they were still crying because they were so upset. Hamish lit the candles and the whole tree shimmered in the candlelight. Everyone gasped in astonishment at the beautiful tree and immediately they began to smile.

'After all,' they said, 'there's still time to buy more presents and redecorate the castle.'

And that's what they did.

December **20**

ALL THOSE TOYS

Jean had been taken to a big shop in the middle of the town by her aunt. There were so many lovely toys there that Jean wanted to play with, that when her aunt's back was turned Jean jumped into an empty packing case and hid until the store was closed. Her poor aunt was very worried about her and called the police. But there was no sign of the little girl, so Jean's aunt assumed she must have gone home.

When the store had closed Jean came out of her hiding place and organized a doll's tea party for all the toys. They were having a wonderful time . . . and then . . .

Two hours later the nightwatchman was astonished to find the little girl sound asleep in a Wendy house.

He phoned the police and Jean was soon fast asleep in her own bed, but not before she had been soundly spanked by her mother.

THE FAN

There was a young lady called Ann
Who was given a beautiful fan;
She held it in place
To cover her face.
And attracted a handsome young man.

He called on her one day for tea
Dressed up in his best finer-ee
He said, 'My sweet dove,
It is you that I love,
Will you please please please marry me?'

She smiled and played with her fan,
And into his arms she then ran.

He held her so tight
She fainted in fright
And died. What a sad end for Ann.

A VISIT TO FATHER CHRISTMAS

John was so excited. His mother had taken him to the big shop in the High Street where they were going to visit Father Christmas.

They queued for quite a long time because there were lots of other boys and girls — all waiting to see Father Christmas.

Eventually it was John's turn. 'What's your name?' asked Father Christmas and when John told him the old man asked

what he wanted for Christmas. John told him that he wanted a rocking horse, a toy car and a big jigsaw puzzle. Each time he said something, Father Christmas repeated it loudly.

And I wonder if John got everything he asked for. He had to wait three whole days before he found out — but I expect he got at least some of them, don't you?

December **23**

WHEN I GROW UP

'When I grow up I'm going to be Queen of the Snow,' said Anne to her friend Clare one day. 'I shall marry the King of the Ice and live in a beautiful castle built of crystals and diamonds. All my dresses shall be shining white and I'll wear fur cloaks.

'I'll drive a sleigh with golden bells on it that ring gently so that all my subjects will know that I'm coming. I'll be the most beautiful queen.'

'Pooh,' laughed Clare. 'It'll be so cold that your nose will be red all the time and you'll have cracked hands. Anyway, I'm going to marry the King of the Spring, and melt your kingdom away.'

'You wouldn't dare,' said Anne.

'I would, but I promise not to if you promise not to marry the King of the Ice and live here.'

' Oh very well,' agreed Anne.

December **24**

UNCLE JOHN'S PRESENT

There was only one thing that Neil wanted for Christmas. It was a toy monkey that he had seen in a toyshop window. He told everyone that that's what he wanted, but he knew that it wasn't in any of the brightly wrapped parcels, because he could see it was still in the toyshop window. The day before Christmas his grandmother gave him a pound note to buy himself something.

Neil ran to the toyshop as fast as possible but when he got there the monkey was gone. 'I am sorry, Neil,' said Mr Harrod, who owned the shop, 'I sold him a few minutes ago to an American.'

Neil walked home sadly. When he got there his mother was very excited. 'Oh Neil,' she cried, 'guess who's just arrived

for Christmas. Your Uncle John from America.'

Neil could see a big man standing behind Mummy. He was wearing a big hat and a yellow tie. Neil smiled and said 'Hello' and went into the living room where the Christmas Tree was.

He looked at the presents and saw a new one had been put there. It had a label on it that said, 'To Neil. Merry Christmas from Uncle John.' I wonder what was in it.

December 25

CHRISTMAS DAY

'Maybe if I creep downstairs and open just one present no one will know,' Michael thought to himself, early one Christmas morning.

His heart was beating hard as his hand opened the living room door where all the presents were. He pushed it open very gently.

'MERRY CHRISTMAS MICHAEL,'

everyone shouted. There were Mummy and Daddy and Granny and Grandpa and the whole family.

'We wanted to surprise you. We knew that you wouldn't be able to resist creeping down and opening a present early.'

Michael and everyone else had such a happy time opening their presents. And everyone loved the presents that Michael had bought with his pocket money for them all, and that made Michael very happy indeed.

Merry Christmas everyone.

December 26

THE RAINY DAY

It was pouring down and Paul the Pixie was sitting in the rain sheltering under his umbrella, waiting for the boat to come and take him across the lake to visit his sister.

He waited and waited, but there was no sign of the boat. Paul began to get quite worried. Perhaps the boatman was

ill or had had an accident. But no, all of a sudden Paul saw the boat coming.

'Where have you been?' Paul asked the boatman when he had clambered aboard. 'You're awfully late.'

'No, I'm not,' said the boatman. 'I always come at exactly twelve o'clock.'

'But it's one o'clock now,' complained Paul, looking at his watch. 'You're an hour late.'

'No, I'm not,' said the boatman, looking at his watch.

'One of us must be wrong,' said Paul. 'I wonder who?'

Well, it turned out that Paul had accidentally put his watch forward by one hour when he had been winding it the night before.

December **27**

THE STAG

A stag went to a pool of clear, cool water one day to have a drink. As he drank he noticed his reflection in the pool.

'I really am incredibly handsome,' he said to himself. 'My antlers are so beautiful. It's such a pity about my spindly legs. I wish I had legs worthy of such a noble head.'

Just then a hunter passed the pool and, seeing the mighty stag, he took out his bow and arrow and shot at the stag. But the stag's fine sense of smell had given him a moment's warning and even as the arrow whizzed past him, the stag was away, running fast on the same spindly legs that he had been so critical of.

When he was out of harm's way the stag again became critical of his appear-

ance. As he mused he wandered into a thicket and his antlers became entwined in the branches of a tree. No matter how he tried he could not free himself.

Suddenly the hunter appeared again and this time his arrow did find its target. It was only as he lay dying that the stag learned his lesson that very often the things we despise most are the things that are most useful to us.

December **28**

THE MAGIC FIREWORK

Gordon had been given a box of fireworks as a Christmas present and he and his father went into the garden to set them off.

There was one firework that suddenly came to life as soon as Gordon lit it. It dazzled and sparkled and spun round and round throwing out jets of glittering colour.

'What are you called?' asked Gordon.

'Catherine,' said the firework. 'I was a girl who believed in Jesus and I was put on trial and found guilty and killed. When fireworks came to Europe some people decided to call one after me, and I still dazzle and glitter and sparkle whenever I am lit.'

'But why?' asked Gordon.

'Because loving Jesus is the most wonderful thing. It makes you really happy to know that he loves you and all you want to do is to tell other people how happy you are.'

December 29

THE PANCAKES

Every year in King David's kingdom each person made a present for his birthday. It was usual that a special dish was made from home-grown food.

One year a girl called June found there was nothing growing in her garden. She had no idea how she would find a present for the prince. She went to ask her wise old grandmother who gave her a basket. When she got home she unpacked it and there were eggs, flour, milk and a pot of jam.

'There's not enough flour to make a cake,' she thought, but she mixed all the ingredients just the same. She poured a little of the mixture into a frying pan and when it was cooked, she wrapped some jam in it and it was delicious. Then she made lots more.

She took them to the king who liked them so much he asked June what they were called.

'Er . . . pancakes, I suppose.' And that's what they are still called today.

December **30**

WHERE'S JANUARY?

The twelve months of the year decided to hold a meeting to discuss who was the most important of them all.

They all arrived at the same time, except for January.

'We can't wait all day for him, let's begin,' said December. 'Although why we're bothering I don't know. I am the most important month. Christmas happens when I am ruling and everyone loves my jolly happy days.'

'Nonsense,' cried August. 'I am much more important. My days are warm and sunny and people relax and are happy when I'm in charge.'

'So what!' blew March. 'I herald spring. When I'm in charge the trees begin to bud and flowers begin to bloom.'

And so the argument raged all day, until October pointed out that they couldn't really decide until January showed up.

'We'd better go and look for him,' suggested May, who was very good-tempered and sweet. And so the eleven months set out to look for January, but there was no sign of him.

After a few hours they all met again and reported. No one had seen a sign of him. Where was January . . .?

Here he comes.

December **31**

ALMOST JANUARY AGAIN!

'We are all important,' said January.

'Without the work we all do none of us could survive. I come first and when I'm ruling things begin to happen under the soil. I prepare the way for February to begin to make things green again. And then March comes and blows away the dust of winter with his strong winds. And then April begins to warm the flowers and plants until May and June take over and everything starts to ripen. Then July and August take over and bring everything to maturity with their long, hot days and warm nights.

'And then September and October come round and the plants are ready to be harvested.

'After all that hard work the people need a rest, so November brings longer nights. And then when people need cheering up, December brings Christmas. You see we're all as important as each other.'